Praise for Lacey's Star

Kay DiBianca's *Lacey's Star* soars to heights of suspense and danger in this intriguing new series. Cassie Deakin is a professional pilot turned reluctant detective who investigates murders in the present that lead to crimes from the distant past. She is a smart, capable, likeable hero in a well-crafted, well-written mystery. I look forward to flying into adventures with Cassie in future books. Highly recommended!

— Debbie Burke, award-winning author of the
Tawny Lindholm Thriller series

An old secret. An unreliable crusader for the truth. Clues that make perfect sense when you put them all together but are indecipherable on their own. Kay DiBianca is hitting her stride as a cozy mystery writer in *Lacey's Star*, the first novel in her new *Lady Pilot in Command* series. DiBianca is well-qualified in the writing and flying departments. If you're looking for a mystery that will grab you and hold you until every question is resolved, *Lacey's Star* is the book you want. DiBianca delivers. Highly recommend!

— LK Simonds, award-winning author of
Stork Bite

D1336333

Lacey's Star

A Lady Pilot in Command Novel

Kay DiBianca

Wordstar Publishing LLC

Published by Wordstar Publishing, LLC.
Memphis, Tennessee

Books may be purchased in quantity and/or special sales by emailing the publisher at wordstar@wordstarpublishing.com.

Cover design by Kristie Koontz.

Lacey's Star / DiBianca —1st ed.

ISBN 978-1-7357888-7-6 (paperback)

ISBN 978-1-7357888-8-3 (ebook)

Library of Congress Control Number: 2023918758

10 9 8 7 6 5 4 3 2 1

1. Fiction 2. Mystery

First Edition printed in the United States of America.

For all the men and women who have served in the United States Armed Forces.

The truth is bitter, but with all its bitterness, it is better than illusion.

— Ahad Ha'Am

You will know the truth, and the truth will set you free.

— The Book of John

Contents

Acknowledgments

I am deeply grateful for the guidance, counsel, love, and support of so many people who helped bring this book to publication:

Good friends and family took the time to read and give feedback on all or part of various drafts. I'm in debt to Jan and Gary Keyes, Debbie Burke, Steve Hooley, Andrew McClurg, Lisa Simonds, Terry Odell, Patricia Bradley, and Tom Throckmorton. I owe special thanks to LtCol (Ret) Mike Ware, Bob Roy (USMC, Vietnam), and Barbara Roy.

Numerous editors, agents, and publishers offered advice and assistance along the way, including Mel Hughes who encouraged me to write this book and provided her developmental editing expertise, and Barbara Curtis, a good friend who supplied copy and line editing with her usual tact and patience.

Additional thanks go to critique group members Ron McMillan, Nick Nixon, and Michael Thompson for their insightful feedback.

Cover designer Kristie Koontz continues to astound me with her "above and beyond" work ethic and the beauty of the book covers she creates.

And, of course, my deepest thanks go to my darling husband, Frank, whose love and support have strengthened me for all these many years.

I also owe thanks to many others who offered encouragement and prayer as I walked through this journey.

I started writing this book with the intention of producing a first-rate mystery. I finished it with a profound sense of gratitude to the men and women who have served in the U.S. Armed Forces and whose sacrifices have helped provide me with the wonderful life I've enjoyed. To all of them: Thank you for your service.

"The Lord is my strength and my shield; in Him my heart trusts, and I am helped; my heart exults, and with my song I give thanks to Him." -- Psalm 28:7

Chapter 1

Taking Off

I do not like handsome men. Not that I have much experience with them, but in my opinion, they're self-absorbed and untrustworthy. Like the one sitting in the passenger seat of my Cessna 172 while I did the run-up prior to takeoff. Frank White.

Frank and I have shared only two experiences in the short time we've known each other. In the first one, I saved his life. In the second, he invited me to dinner and stood me up.

Now I'm not generally a person to hold a grudge, but being stood up is on my short list of unforgivable sins. So, when the company I worked for informed me I *had* to fly Frank to a meeting at my uncle's farm a couple of hundred miles away, I turned my face into stone and took the assignment.

If Frank noticed my icy silence as I did the pre-flight check, he didn't let on. Out of the corner of my eye, I saw the little smirk on his face while he scrolled on his phone, his dark hair hanging down on his forehead. He needed a haircut.

The Newton Airport tower called down. "Cessna Three One

Four Bravo Charlie, you're cleared for takeoff on runway three-six." After a brief pause, he added, "Have a nice flight, Cassie."

Frank adjusted his headset when he heard the call from the tower and winked at me. I gave him a look I reserve only for the lowest forms of human life and focused my attention back on the flight panel.

"Roger that," I said and repeated the instructions back to the air traffic controller. Then I added power and maneuvered Scout onto the end of the runway. Scout is the name I use for the little blue and white Cessna that was my father's pride and joy. He taught me how to fly when I was a young girl, and he left the plane to me when he died.

My frustration evaporated as my aircraft responded to full power and accelerated down the runway. When we reached sixty knots, I gently pulled back the yoke, the nose lifted, and in one breathless moment, we were free from the earth.

This was a feeling I could never get enough of—the thrill of release as I watched the ground drop away. We climbed over the end of the runway, and meadows of goldenrod waved goodbye as we soared into blue heaven.

When we reached eight thousand feet, air traffic control directed me to change to compass heading two-seven-zero, so I made the turn and we were wings level, sailing west, with the early morning sun at our backs.

Frank shoved his phone into his pants pocket. "Can I talk now?" he said with a little smile that showed the dimple in his left cheek. He knew full well that we had reached our altitude, allowing him to talk.

"Let's get one thing straight," I huffed out. "I didn't want to take this flight, but Michael insisted, and my contract with the corporation says I have to provide flying services when requested by the owner." I gulped in a lungful of air and put some authority in my voice. "This is the last place on earth I want to be."

"Technically speaking," he said and blinked at me, "we're not on the earth right now."

That's another thing I don't like about him. He makes me feel foolish. I pressed my lips together and bit back the retort that was trying to make its way out.

"I didn't want to contact you," he continued, "but Sheriff Buchanan specifically asked if you were interested."

I plastered a bored expression on my face and looked at him. "I don't care whose idea it was. There is nothing in the entire world that could convince me to join your law enforcement team." I yawned for effect. "I value my life."

"I know that, Cassie, and just for the record, I don't think you should join. I wouldn't want to put you in danger." His eyebrows wrinkled with concern, but then he gave that little grin. "You'd make a great team member, though. We need good pilots."

"Never." I said it with enough emphasis that he wouldn't ask again.

Frank leaned his head back on the headrest. "Okay, I get the message. Wake me when we get there."

I'd been hired to fly Frank to my Uncle Charlie's farm in Tabor County. Apparently, the sheriff there had some concerns about crime in the area, and Frank was tapped to interview my uncle about safety issues in the farming community.

I couldn't quite figure out Frank's job. When I first met him, he was a DEA agent, but today he told me he resigned that position to join the sheriff's department in Tabor County.

I glanced over at him. Why would he leave the DEA to become a deputy sheriff in northwest Nevada nowheresville? Seemed like a step down to me.

But that was none of my business. All I had to do was fly him to my uncle's farm and wait around until he finished the interview. Besides, I didn't want to think about Frank White when I could soak up the joy of flying over the magnificent countryside that lay beneath us.

The western United States was born out of a tectonic shift that lifted the Rockies into existence and carved the farmlands, deserts, and canyons. The yin and yang of that geologic event produced a landscape so stunning that it never ceased to startle me with its raw, untamed beauty.

While Frank slept, we flew over the foothills and into the wide plain, past rock formations and gullies, over wadis and wastelands, toward western Nevada and the fertile spread of alfalfa fields dotted with herds of cattle.

We made good time with the wind at our back, and I started my descent when we got within ten miles of the farm.

Uncle Charlie and I have always been close. Good thing since he's my only living relative. Whenever I fly into his place, I drop down and circle the farmhouse a couple of times so he can hear the whine of Scout's engine. Wherever he is, Uncle Charlie leaves what he's doing, runs out, and stands by the old well in front of the house. The sight of big Uncle Charlie in his trademark dark blue flannel shirt and denim overalls waving like a crazy man always makes me happy.

I descended to a few hundred feet above ground level and did two circles around the farmhouse, but Uncle Charlie didn't appear. That was odd.

I dropped the flaps and slowed the airspeed for the final approach. It was another dry August day, and the recent drought had made the ground hard. When my little plane settled down onto the strip of parched yellow grass in front of the house, Frank opened his eyes. "Are we here?" he asked, and I swallowed a sarcastic reply. I would not let him spoil the good vibes I always had when I visited my uncle.

By the time I shut the engine down, released my seat belt, and climbed out, Frank had come around to my side of the aircraft. He took my arm, but his face was crumpled into a strange frown. I tried to pull away, but his grip tightened.

"Hold it, Cassie," he said and pulled the Glock out from under his jacket.

Chapter 2

The Farm

"What the heck?" This was over the top, even for Frank. "What are you doing?"

Frank's mouth pinched into a straight line, and his voice dropped to just above a whisper. "Do you know how to handle a gun?"

"Of course I do. I was raised in Texas."

He let go of my arm, lifted his pant leg, and unhooked a .38 that was strapped there. What was this guy? A one-man arms warehouse? He handed it to me. "Don't even think about firing it unless I tell you."

He didn't have to worry about me going all John Wayne. I hate guns, and I made sure to point this one at the ground.

Frank gestured to the grass in front of the plane where there was a dark red stain. "Blood," he said.

"Blood? Uncle Charlie!" I started to move away, but he grabbed my arm again and jerked me back with a vengeance.

"I'm going to check the house," he said. "Stay here."

"No way I'm staying out here." I yanked my arm out of his grasp so hard he couldn't argue.

We moved up to the house and crept across the front porch. Frank motioned for me to take a position on the right side of the front door while he stood on the left. He pulled the screen door open and swung it for me to hold.

I didn't realize I was biting my lower lip until I tasted the warm blood. I wiped my sleeve across my mouth and held my breath.

Frank banged on the door with the butt of his gun. "Open up. Law Enforcement," he yelled. You could have heard him five miles away, but there was no sound coming from inside. He banged again. "Open the door. *Now.*" Still, nothing moved.

If Uncle Charlie had been awake and able to move, there would have been a lot of noise. Uncle Charlie is kind of clumsy. It runs in the Deakin family. If he walks across a room, he can usually find a way to knock a lamp off a table or trip over the edge of a rug and bang his knee into something. And if he does hurt himself, he usually shouts a few words of farmhand wisdom to acknowledge the fact. But there wasn't a sound. Except for my heart pounding against my rib cage.

Frank motioned to me that he would go in, but I should stay on the porch. I shook my head and glared at him. Whatever happened, I was going to be right behind him.

He put his hand on the doorknob, turned it quietly, and then kicked the door so hard it flew open and banged into an end table.

Frank barged in, his gun held two-handed in front of him. He swung around in all directions and then cocked his head for me to follow. I moved in behind him.

The large, comfortable living room that I had always loved, with its stone fireplace and leather couches, looked the same as always. Farm magazines lay scattered on the coffee table and sofa. A picture of my dad and me standing in front of Scout was on the mantel, and I caught a hint of cigar smoke. Uncle Charlie liked his occasional stogie.

"Charlie!" Frank called out at the top of his lungs. "Charlie. Are you here?"

We crept from room to room, with Frank leading the way, but the only sounds we heard were the occasional creaks and groans of the old hardwood floors. Every room was a testimony to Uncle Charlie's bachelor-disheveled chaos. As we crossed each threshold, my eyes scanned quickly for him, but he wasn't there. Thankfully, I didn't see any blood either.

Finally, we got to the kitchen. The red light on the coffee maker glowed and the aroma of Uncle Charlie's favorite dark roast hung in the air. There was a half-full mug of coffee on the table and part of an English muffin, but no sign of a struggle. Frank let his Glock fall to his side and ran a hand through his hair. "Maybe your uncle left to go into town," he said.

"No way. His truck is outside. Besides, he knew I was coming. He'd never leave."

"Does your uncle keep any valuables on the premises? Money? Anything that robbers would be interested in?"

I tried to look like I was thinking about it, but I had promised Uncle Charlie I wouldn't tell anyone about the secret he let me in on a few days earlier. There was no way I'd break a promise to Uncle Charlie, so I made a non-committal "Hmmm" and left it at that.

That seemed to satisfy Frank. "Well," he said, "it doesn't look like there was a struggle. Maybe somebody came to the door, and he thought it was you."

"If he heard something and thought it was me, he would have gone out to ..." I felt a cold knife cut through my chest. "The well. That's where he always stands when I come to the house." I raced out the front door.

Frank caught me before I got to the well and held me back. "I'll look." He peered over the side of the stone wall, then turned back to me. "It's okay. There's nothing there."

I ran to his side to see for myself. The reflection of the sun glinted off the water at the bottom of the well.

"Let's take a look in the barn," he said.

Frank's gun was still drawn as we made our way back through the house and along the side of the barn. I took a deep breath. The smell of the horses and fresh hay sent me back to my childhood and gave me a sense of security. There couldn't be anything wrong here. Maybe one of the horses got injured. That would explain the blood. Frank was probably overreacting because he's law enforcement, and they always think the worst.

I had talked myself into thinking there was a perfectly good explanation for everything. As we rounded the corner of the barn, Frank stopped so quickly I slammed into his back. He put his arm out as if to shield me, but from where I stood, I could see something sticking out from inside the barn. It was a man's leg.

Chapter 3

Uncle Charlie

He was lying on his back with his arms splayed out and a big, ugly hole in his chest. There was a lot of blood.

I saw just enough to know it wasn't Uncle Charlie. I turned away and ran back to the corner of the house where there was a water spigot. I splashed cold water on my face and tried to forget what I had seen. Frank followed me.

He put his hand on my back and leaned in. "You okay?"

"Yes," I said. "I— I've never seen anything like that before." I ran water into my cupped hand and took a swallow.

"Take a couple of deep breaths," he said and handed me his handkerchief. "Do you know him?"

"I didn't get a good look at his face."

"Think you can try again?"

I clenched my teeth and took a few more deep breaths. Once I knew what a horrible death looked like, I thought maybe I could take it, so I turned off the spigot, and we walked back to the door of the barn.

I glanced at the dead man's face and quickly twisted away. "I never saw him before." I felt my stomach turning somersaults while Frank called 911.

I heard the distinctive whinny of Old Dan coming from inside the barn. Dan was the gigantic gelding Uncle Charlie had raised from a little colt, and the old horse was almost like a dog in his devotion to my uncle.

As my eyes adjusted to the dark, I made out Old Dan standing inside the main aisle of the barn, beside a big lump of something next to one of the horse stalls. At first, I thought it was a horse blanket, but then I spotted the blue flannel shirt. "Uncle Charlie!" I sprinted around the dead man and raced down the aisle of the barn to kneel beside my beloved uncle.

He was lying on his side on the dirt floor, but his face was turned toward me, and I could see him breathing. There was blood pooled around his left shoulder.

Frank ran to me. "Don't move him," he said. His line was still open to 911, and he ordered them to send an ambulance. He placed his fingers on Uncle Charlie's neck, checking his pulse. "Stay with your uncle," he said. "I'm going to check the toolshed."

Frank left, and I put my hand on Uncle Charlie's cheek. It was warm. "It's me, Uncle Charlie. It's Cassie."

His eyelids fluttered and barely opened. "Don't cry, little girl," he whispered. Then he moaned and his eyes rolled back.

Little girl. That's what Uncle Charlie called me when I was growing up. Even after I reached my adult height of five feet, nine inches, I was still his little girl, and he was always my big Uncle Charlie.

Frank reappeared. "The toolshed is locked. I don't see any sign of a struggle out there." He put his hand on my shoulder. "Keep him quiet. I want to check the rest of the scene."

Frank walked down the center aisle of the barn, gun drawn, looking in each of the horse stalls. Then he circled around the side, behind each of the stalls where Uncle Charlie kept supplies. He climbed over bales of hay and straw and made his way back to the main aisle.

He approached the tack room, which was set at the far end of the barn behind a closed door. He put one hand on the knob and shoved the door open, his Glock pointed firmly in front of him. I held my breath as he disappeared inside.

The .38 was lying on the ground next to me. I picked it up and stood. As much as I hated the feeling of that metal in my hand, I knew I'd use it if I had to. After a minute, Frank came out of the tack room and walked toward me.

"I don't think there's anybody here, but be on your guard. There're a lot of places to hide."

Old Dan whinnied and dropped his head down to nuzzle Uncle Charlie. "We need to put the horse back in his stall," Frank took Dan's lead line and pulled on it to turn Dan around, but the old horse stood firm.

"He won't go with you if you try to take him away from Uncle Charlie," I said. "He doesn't know you."

"Will he go with you?"

Old Dan and I were well acquainted. He was the first horse I had ever ridden, and I spent a lot of my childhood on his back. "C'mon, fella." Dan turned easily when I gave the lead line a gentle tug. "Let's get you put away so we can take care of our uncle." He followed me into the stall.

I unhooked the lead line and patted the old gelding's neck. "He'll be okay," I said as if Dan could understand. I stepped back out into the aisle. "I don't know why there's a lead line on Dan. Uncle Charlie told me he never uses one on him."

"Hang it on the wall. Maybe we'll learn something from it," Frank said.

I knelt beside my uncle again and stroked his cheek.

The sound of a siren split the air, and Frank put his gun away. "I'll go meet the ambulance and direct them into the barn. You go to the hospital with your uncle, and I'll wait here for the sheriff's team." He hustled down the aisle and out of the barn.

Uncle Charlie moaned, and I leaned down close to his ear. "The secret," I whispered.

He barely shook his head, and his voice was so low I could hardly make it out. "No."

"Be still," I said. "The ambulance is here. You're going to be all right."

He closed his eyes while I stroked his hair and whispered again, "It's all going to be all right."

Chapter 4

The Hospital

The Bridgeton Hospital emergency room doors slid aside, and the ambulance guys rushed Uncle Charlie's gurney down a hall that had a strong odor of antiseptic. I followed at a run.

They rolled him into a side room, but a tall, horse-faced nurse stopped me at the door. Nurse Ratched, no doubt, and she had an attitude to match. She stretched her arm out over the doorway and stared me down with dull gray eyes. "He's being taken to surgery. You can't go in. We'll let you know his status as soon as we can."

"But I need to stay with him." I tried to make my voice sound like I was in charge.

She just shook her head. Her eyes scanned my clothes, and I realized what a mess I must be. She pointed to a room across the hall. "You can clean up in there."

Standing in the bright light of the ladies' bathroom, I stared at my image in the mirror. My dark brown ponytail had come loose and tangled hair fell around my face.

The air corporation I fly for insists on a professional look in the pilots, so I always wear a white blouse and navy blue slacks when

I'm flying passengers. Now my white blouse had blood and dirt stains, and my slacks were in the same condition.

I washed my face and hands and retied my hair into a ponytail. While I dried my hands, I looked back at my reflection, remembering the way Uncle Charlie used to tease me that I had sapphires for eyes. There was nothing sparkly about the way I looked now.

I was empty inside, like some big alien had sucked the organs out, and all that was left was a hollow shell. I had only felt that way once before—at my dad's funeral. Something had been taken away that could never be replaced, and there was nothing I could do about it.

"Pray, Cassie." That's what our neighbor, Mrs. Greenway, said when she saw how despondent I was after Dad's death. "Sometimes all we have is prayer," she'd say. So I prayed then, and I prayed again while I leaned on the bathroom sink. But this time there was anger in my words. "How could you let this happen?" I said out loud.

I went back out to the corridor and paced back and forth until the emergency room doctor came out. He was tall with a kind expression and massively large hands. "I'm Dr. Dudley," he said as he lowered his mask to speak. "Your uncle has lost a lot of blood. We need to transfuse him, but we're very short on blood here. Any chance you're the same blood type?"

I had no idea, but they took a sample of my blood. It matched, so they drained a lot out of me and set me up in a recovery area to rest and worry.

I lay on the bed and checked my watch. It was only ten o'clock in the morning, but I felt like an entire week had passed since we left the airport in Newton.

The room was dark. I felt slightly dizzy, and my head slumped back against the pillow.

I heard a voice. It was Uncle Charlie. "Run, Cassie. Quick.

Run and hide." I was standing in a forest. There were gigantic trees all around and a little path. I could hear Uncle Charlie, but I couldn't see him. "Run, little girl." I was frozen in place. There was no one to help me. I was alone. I looked around at the forest that was closing in. My heart was pounding, but I couldn't move. Then I felt a hand on my shoulder.

My eyes flew open, and I jerked awake. Frank was standing next to the bed with his hand on my shoulder. He was frowning.

"Uncle Charlie!" I shouted and moved to get up.

Frank gently pushed me back on the pillow and held me down. "He's still in surgery," he said. "The nurse says you need to lie still."

I wiped at the perspiration on my forehead, ashamed that I had fallen asleep while Uncle Charlie was still in danger. "I need to find out how he's doing." I tried to move again, but Frank was still holding me down.

"Uh-uh. You need to rest. The nurse told me they took five hundred milliliters of blood, and you're not to get up for an hour." He checked his own watch. "You still have a few minutes on the clock." His eyes were dark with concern. "I asked about your uncle. They say he's in great shape for a man his age, and they expect him to pull through."

Tears stung my eyes.

"I brought you this." Frank held up the overnight bag that I always kept in the plane.

"Thanks." I pulled the bag onto my midsection and hugged it. Something to hold on to. "Tell me what you found at the farm."

The muscles on the side of his face twitched. "I called in the local authorities, and I stayed at the scene for a while. They're still there, dusting for fingerprints, checking for DNA, and looking for clues."

"Do they know who the dead man was?"

"Not yet. There wasn't any ID on him, but they'll fingerprint the body, check the DNA against the national databases, and we should know soon." He gave me an almost-smile. "There's somebody here to see you if you're up to it."

Somebody to see me? I nodded, but I didn't know anybody around this place except Uncle Charlie. Frank got up, opened the door, and motioned to someone.

A man peeked around the corner and then moved fully into my view. He was so big, he seemed to take up all the free space in the recovery room. Arms covered with tattoos and gray hair blown in all directions, he was holding a biker's helmet in one hand, and gave me a wave with the other. "Well, hello, little sister," he said.

"Ralph!"

Chapter 5

Ralph

Ralph ambled in and dropped his helmet on the chair next to the bed. He likes to call me "little sister" even though we're not related. Now he was here, looking all concerned.

He put his hand on the edge of the mattress and leaned over, looking into my face. "Sorry to hear what happened."

Ralph owns a little country store out in the middle of the desert, between nothing and nowhere. He and his biker friends were involved in that one adventure I had with Frank. I had dropped Frank off at an old, abandoned airport hangar that was a few miles south of Ralph's place. Frank and his partner were planning a sting operation on some drug kingpins, but the whole thing had gone sideways.

In the end, I had dropped a one-gallon can of Sherwin-Williams Red Barn paint out of my airplane onto the windshield of a moving car where the bad guys had Frank tied up. When the car screeched to a stop in front of Ralph's place, he and his buddies rescued Frank.

Frank stepped up beside the bed. "Hope you don't mind,

Cassie. While you came to the hospital in the ambulance, I flew your plane over to Ralph's to see if any of the guys could help us. Ralph didn't have any customers, so he was good enough to close up shop and come back with me. We loaded one of his motorcycles in the back of your plane."

My brain was still in a fog. "Why did you think Ralph could help?"

"There were motorcycle tracks at your uncle's place."

"Motorcycles?" I had grown to love the bikers who helped me before, and I didn't want to believe bikers would do such a terrible thing. "Bikers did that to Uncle Charlie?"

Ralph nodded. "That's what they tell me. I haven't seen the place yet, but I don't doubt the authorities around here know what motorcycle tracks look like." Ralph pressed his lips together. "Frank thinks I might be able to help. He wants me to take a look at the dead man."

"Oh." I felt a lump in my throat. "You don't think it could be one of the guys who hang out at your place, do you?"

"Don't know. I'm gonna head over to the morgue now, but I wanted to come here first to see how you were doing." He put his hand on my arm. "You okay?"

"I guess."

"Well, you hang loose, little sister. I'll let you know what I find out." He picked up his helmet from the chair. "Cassie, what in the world would people be after at your uncle's farm?"

I shrugged and turned away, determined to keep my uncle's secret until I could talk to him.

Ralph walked to the door, but then he turned back and pointed at Frank. "You take care of her," he said and left.

Frank stood over the bed and grinned at me for the first time since we flew into this mess. "I guess you're my responsibility now."

I scowled back. "I can take care of myself." I brushed a lock of hair out of my face. "All I want is a hot shower."

He dropped the grin. "Maybe later, but first I have to ask you some questions that might help us figure out what happened to your uncle."

"Like what?"

"Did he have a girlfriend?"

I laughed out loud. Uncle Charlie with a woman? "No. He's a confirmed bachelor. My dad told me Uncle Charlie got his heart broken when he was young and swore off all women after that. And I don't think any woman would be interested in him either. His idea of a good time is farming and taking care of his horses."

Frank looked really interested in what I had to say. "You sure about that?"

"About what? Women or horses?"

"Women. Or maybe just one woman." Frank kept his eyes on my face.

"What are you getting at?"

"We found some things in your uncle's house that make us think he had a girlfriend."

I sat up. "What things?"

"We found an eyelash curler in one of the bathrooms and a woman's pink, frilly nightgown in one of the closets. From what you told us about your uncle, I doubt he's a cross-dresser." He tilted his head to one side and his brown eyes twinkled. "Maybe you left those things there when you visited him?"

I realized my mouth was hanging open, and I closed it. "I don't own a pink, frilly nightgown," I said and felt my face flush. "And I wouldn't even know how to use an eyelash curler."

"So it appears your uncle does have a girlfriend."

"Impossible. Uncle Charlie wouldn't keep secrets from me."

Frank shrugged. "Maybe this is a new relationship and he just hadn't gotten around to telling you."

"You don't know him."

"I know he's a man, Cassie. And now I know there may be someone very close to him who could have information that we can use. We have to find her. Any help you can provide will be important."

I shook my head. "I'm clueless. The only woman I've seen around the farm is Dr. Washburn. She's the vet who takes care of the horses."

"Maybe she's his girlfriend. What's she like?"

"About eighty years old, a face like a prune and an attitude to match. She wears a tattered old straw hat that must be as old as she is. And I don't see her using an eyelash curler."

"You never know about women," Frank said and arched one eyebrow.

I glared at him. "There's got to be another explanation."

"I can't wait to hear what that is." He checked his watch. "In the meantime, you should be able to get up now. Why don't you wash up and come on out in the hall? I think they have a little cafeteria here. We'll get something to eat and talk about the girlfriend."

Chapter 6

Mandy

Frank left the room to wait in the hall, and I took the overnight bag he had brought me into the tiny bathroom. It felt wonderful to get out of my dirty clothes. I washed up and changed into a clean T-shirt and jeans. I rummaged around in the bag, found my Nikes, and pulled them on. Then I packed my soiled laundry into the duffel bag.

Frank was sitting on the bench across the hall, frowning and scrolling his phone. He looked up when I opened the door, and his expression relaxed. He actually smiled.

He had changed from his dress clothes into a faded blue T-shirt that strained to cover his chest and arms, and he had on jeans that looked like they were molded to him. He must work out every day. I hated that my stomach did a flip-flop when he stood and walked toward me. I reminded myself how much I don't like handsome men. Especially one with a perfect build.

He walked to my side and looked down at me. I noticed his dark brown eyes had flecks of gold in them. Frank must be about six feet tall, but with the cowboy boots, he was even taller. I made a mental note to buy myself a pair of boots.

He touched my elbow. "Are you okay?" he asked without the usual smirk.

"Of course," I said and tried to sound confident.

"I just talked to the operating room nurse," he said. "It'll be another hour or so before he's out of surgery. Let's get something to eat."

Just then, a young woman dressed in a pink-striped uniform rolled a cart filled with snacks around the corner toward us. She had long blonde hair and a face caked with makeup. She stopped in front of Frank and batted mascara-laden lashes at him like she was waving.

"Well, hello!" she said with more enthusiasm than a simple greeting required. "I've never seen you here before. Who are you?" I guess they don't teach modesty anymore in charm school.

Frank gave her his patented look, complete with slow, crooked grin. "Hey. I'm Frank," he said. "Who are you?"

She leaned against the cart and threw one hip out. "I'm available," she said and squeaked out a high-pitched giggle to go with it. She looked like she thought that was the cleverest remark ever, and I considered going back into the room and throwing up.

She tossed her hair back. "My name's Amanda," she said, "but everybody calls me Mandy." How appropriate. Mandy the candy-striper.

"Well, Mandy," Frank said and put a little too much emphasis on the name for my taste. "We'd like to find the cafeteria. Can you direct us?"

She looked like he'd just asked her to the prom. She let go of the cart and slithered over to Frank's side. "Just go right down that hall." She pointed to the one with the sign that said Cafeteria.

Frank smiled at her like she had given him the answer to some fundamental question of life. "Thanks, Mandy," he said. I rolled my eyes toward the ceiling.

"Anytime you need anything at all, you just come see me," she said, and I wondered if she was going to jump him right there.

"Candy-striper!" Mercifully, a voice interrupted her come-on before she lost complete control. It was Nurse Ratched at the other end of the hall. "Bring the cart down here," she ordered. I silently thanked Ratched as Mandy flounced away, looking back over her shoulder at Frank. There was more in that look than just a friendly goodbye.

Frank caught up with me as I headed toward the cafeteria. "Look, Cassie," he leaned over and whispered. "It's a good idea to be nice to people. You never know who can help us."

"She looked pretty eager to help you," I said and regretted the tone of my voice right away. I felt constantly off-balance around Frank, being snarky and saying the wrong things. I had always been the nice girl, unruffled and responsible, and I didn't like sounding mean and envious.

We found the cafeteria right where the sign said it was. It actually had some pretty good hot food, and I was famished. I hadn't had anything to eat that morning because I thought I'd have breakfast at Uncle Charlie's. We got our meals, settled at one of the tables, and I tore into my scrambled eggs.

Frank was making good progress on a roast beef sandwich. Between bites, he said, "Let's get back to the woman your uncle was seeing."

I wanted to argue that Uncle Charlie didn't have a girlfriend, but the evidence they found must add up to something.

"You don't remember him telling you anything about her?" he said.

"Nothing. All we ever talked about was family, horses, airplanes, stuff like that. He never once said he had a girlfriend."

"Did he ever mention that he met some new friends? You know, maybe there's a group he hangs out with that she's in and they got cozy."

I couldn't see Uncle Charlie getting "cozy" with a woman. Especially a woman who uses an eyelash curler.

I shook my head and took a bite of hash browns. "I know there are some farmers who get together to talk about the weather, the price of fertilizer, and that kind of stuff. I drive into Millers Ridge with Uncle Charlie now and then when he meets with some friends there."

"Were there any women?"

I stopped chewing and tried to remember. "No. I'm sure I'd remember that."

"Then it must be something recent. We'll get all the information we can from the crime scene. We might be able to tell something about her, like her shoe size or hair color."

I couldn't resist. "You don't suppose she was a blonde, do you?" I opened my eyes wide and blinked at him like Mandy had done.

Frank smirked back at me. "We'll see."

We were finishing up our meals when Nurse Ratched appeared. Uncle Charlie was out of surgery, and they were taking him to recovery. I crammed the last morsel of toast in my mouth, gulped down the rest of my coffee, and headed for the door.

Chapter 7

Recovery

D r. Dudley met us just outside Uncle Charlie's room. "The operation went well," he said, "but your uncle has a head injury in addition to the gunshot wound. It's possible someone attacked him with a blunt object, or maybe he fell and hit his head when he was shot. I've given him a heavy dose of sedatives. We want to reduce the risk of him moving around." He pulled off his surgical cap. "Don't worry. He'll be all right."

I appreciated the gesture, but my nerves were on high alert as Frank and I went into the room. Uncle Charlie was lying flat on his back, eyes closed and tubes going into his arm. His usual ruddy complexion was pale, and he looked smaller than I remembered. Hard to think of this man-giant as being little.

I held his hand, half expecting him to open his eyes and smile at me, but there was no response. I looked at the nurse who was fussing with some of the equipment that was beeping and blipping on the other side of the bed.

She repeated what the doctor said. "He's heavily sedated."

"Do you know when he'll wake up?" I asked.

"The doctor wants him sedated until tomorrow morning." She

gave me a sympathetic look. "You're tired. Why don't you go home and get some rest? There's nothing you can do for your uncle now. He's in good hands." She finished her work and left the room.

I squeezed Uncle Charlie's hand, but there was still no response, and I wondered if I'd ever see him open his eyes or laugh or ...

I felt Frank's presence right behind me. "I'm sorry you have to go through this, Cassie. I know it must be really hard."

I turned on him. How could he understand what it felt like when the last person in the world who loved me might die? "You don't know anything." I shoved my index finger at his chest. "Uncle Charlie is my only living relative. He's my father's brother. He helped raise me, and he loved me." I bit my lip. "You don't know what it's like to be left alone."

Frank put his hands on my shoulders and held them in a firm grip. "I do know what it's like, Cassie. I know exactly what it's like."

I pulled back and looked into his face. There was a dark gloom about his eyes. "What—"

The door pushed open, and Ralph barged in. "Oh, sorry," he said when he saw us standing there like that. "I'll come back."

"No. It's all right." Frank released me and stepped back.

Ralph came over to the bed. "So this is your Uncle Charlie? He looks like a good man."

"He is." I sniffed and pulled a Kleenex out of the box on the side table. "Did you find out anything about the dead man?"

"No." Ralph turned to look at Frank. "I didn't recognize him."

"Any chance he may have come to your place?" Frank asked.

"I don't remember everybody who shows up, but he doesn't look familiar."

Frank rubbed his chin. "I'm sure we'll get an ID from finger-prints or DNA." He turned to me. "Cassie, do you mind if I borrow your plane and take it back to the farm?"

"Why?"

"I want to take another look around. Ralph, why don't you come along? Maybe you can help us identify something about the tire tracks."

"Yeah. I'll take my bike and meet you there." Ralph put his arm around me. "Now don't you worry, little sister, everything's gonna be just fine. Old Ralph here will make sure of it."

"I'm going too. There's no sense in staying here. Uncle Charlie won't regain consciousness until tomorrow. I'll leave my phone number in case they need to call me."

Frank looked skeptical. "I'd rather you stayed here, Cassie."

"No way." I grabbed my jacket and headed for the door.

Chapter 8

Ruddy

Frank insisted I had been through too much trauma to fly, so he took command of Scout. It was a short flight back to Uncle Charlie's farm, and it was early afternoon when we touched down. The sun was high in the sky and the ground was still hard and dry.

Frank landed farther out than we had before so he wouldn't spoil the crime scene any more than we already had. We climbed out and walked toward the front of the house.

"There." Frank pointed to the ground where he had first spotted blood. A woman was kneeling over the site, collecting some of the grass. Ralph was standing next to her.

"Hey, Bailey," Frank said. "How's it going?"

"Good." She stood. She looked to be in her forties, maybe early fifties. Even though she was tiny—I would guess shorter than five feet—she had a no-nonsense look about her that made me think she knew what she was doing. When Frank introduced us and explained it was my uncle's place, she shook her head. "Sorry to hear it," she said. "How is he?"

"He'll pull through." I sounded more confident than I felt. "He's a tough old bird."

"Good to hear." She held up several plastic bags of blood-stained grass clippings. "I got samples of the blood here. We'll check against the corpse and Cassie's uncle. It may belong to one of them, or we may have a third shooting victim."

"Thanks, Bailey," Frank said and turned to Ralph. "Any idea about the tires?"

"The ground is hard, so the prints aren't great, but it looks like a Dunlop tire tread. They make one specifically for Harleys. I want to look farther out to see if I can get a better print."

"Great. How many motorcycles do you figure there were?"

Bailey pointed toward the area where Frank had first spotted the blood. "There was just one bike probably parked there. The blood trail stops here." She pointed with her boot. "Looks like somebody got shot and made it back to the motorcycle and took off."

"We know one guy didn't make it back to the bike, so it looks like there were two men who came on one motorcycle," Frank said.

"Yes." Bailey pointed to the tracks leading up to the blood. "You can see the bike tracks are deeper up to where it was parked. They're lighter going off in that direction." She waved her arm in the other direction.

"But what did they want? Why attack Charlie Deakin?" Frank scratched his chin.

Bailey shrugged. "That'll be up to you guys and Ruddy to figure out."

"Who's Ruddy?" I asked.

"Ask him." She pointed to Frank. "He works for Ruddy now."

"Well, well." A deep voice barked from behind me. "First day on the job, and you already missed a meeting and landed in the middle of a murder."

I turned to see a man striding toward us from the front of the house. He was wearing a white dress shirt with a bolo tie, blue jeans, and cowboy boots. His Stetson was beige and looked like it had spent its best years in the rough western terrain. And there was a sheriff's star fastened to his belt.

He walked right up to Frank and looked at him like he was reading his mind. Or maybe his soul. They were about the same height, and Frank stood still for several seconds until, finally, he held his hand out.

"Frank White, reporting for duty."

I had the same feeling I get watching a National Geographic special on mountain goats getting ready to have a go at each other. When they shook hands, I saw the veins on Frank's fist stand out.

They stood locked in the handshake for several seconds. It looked to me like some kind of weird male bonding ritual. When they finally unhooked, the sheriff gave a brief nod. "It's good to have you aboard, Frank."

"It's an honor, sir," Frank replied.

Women would never be so obvious when they sized each other up. We're more subtle.

Frank turned to me. "Cassie Deakin, this is Ruddy Buchanan. Ruddy is the sheriff of Tabor County. I'm his new deputy."

Sheriff Buchanan turned his attention to me. His face looked like it had been carved out of granite, all sharp planes and angles. It gave him an alpha-male look that went well with the non-smile. "Cassie Deakin, eh? You must be the pilot I hear so much about." His eyes flitted to Frank and then back to me. "They tell me you're excellent at what you do." He tilted his head just slightly and looked at me with hazel-colored eyes, as if he was trying to read my thoughts.

I'm normally a very polite person, but I was tired and upset about Uncle Charlie. "I wouldn't believe everything I hear if I were you," I retorted.

He raised his eyebrows. "With that attitude, young lady ..." He paused like he was going to give me a lecture, and I braced myself. But then the edges of his mouth turned up, and he said, "... you'd make a good cop."

Chapter 9

Greg

Frank introduced Ralph. While Ralph and Sheriff Buchanan examined the motorcycle tracks, Frank and I walked back to the barn.

"Sheriff Buchanan seems like an interesting guy," I said as we retraced our path along the side of the barn.

"The word 'interesting' doesn't even begin to describe him," Frank said. "They tell me he was a psychology major in college. When I interviewed with him a month ago, he gave me one heck of a psychological workout. He asked me everything from my experience at DEA to how many books I read each year and what were my favorite video games." Frank shook his head. "He has a way of staring at you that makes you feel like he knows the answers even before he asks the questions."

"The way you two looked at each other, I thought you hadn't met before."

"I initially met him when I had the interview, but this is my first official day on the job." He grimaced and rubbed his knuckles. "That was a welcoming handshake."

We rounded the corner of the barn the way we'd done that morning and came to the place where we had found the body.

A tall, skinny guy wearing a gray baseball cap stood over the blood-stained ground. The left side of his face showed a deep scar from his hairline down to his chin. It made his mouth twist a little to one side when he looked around and smiled at us.

"Hey, Greg." Frank nodded and gestured toward me. "This is Cassie Deakin. Cassie, meet Greg Larsen. The best forensics guy in the state."

Greg tipped his hat at me. "Sorry to hear about your uncle. I hope he's gonna make it."

"Thank you."

Frank peered down at the ground next to Greg's feet. "Finding anything interesting?"

"Maybe. We had a chance to examine the body before they took him to the morgue. Looks like one shot from a very big gun. Close range." He pointed away from the barn.

"So the shot didn't come from inside the barn?" I asked.

"No. Obvious exit wound on the back. He must have been dead before he hit the ground."

"My uncle was inside the barn," I said, "so he couldn't have been the one who shot this guy."

"Any clues?" Frank asked.

"One very interesting one," Greg said. "Both his legs were broken, like he'd been hit with something hard."

"That's strange. Any theories about how it all went down?"

"Just a wild guess," Greg said. "Several guys come here looking for something—maybe money or drugs. Maybe something else. When they leave, there's a scuffle. Cassie's uncle gets off a shot and wounds one or two of them. When they leave, one of the guys decides he's gonna keep the entire stash for himself and offs this one."

"Plausible," Frank said. "But how did his legs get broken?"

"That's a mystery," Greg said.

"I think I know how that happened," I said and watched while expressions of masculine disbelief crossed both their faces. I truly love moments like those.

"How could you know?" Greg asked.

I walked back into the barn and got Old Dan out of his stall. I brought him out to where Frank and Greg stood side-by-side, staring at me. "Dan was loose when we got here. I'm guessing he tried to protect Uncle Charlie."

Greg looked down at the big gelding's hooves. "Well, I'll be," he said. "Look, Frank. There's blood on the horse's hooves. You think he stomped the guy we found?" he asked me.

"I sure would pity anybody who tried to hurt Uncle Charlie while Dan was around." I gave the old gelding a pat on the neck.

Greg used a small tool to scrape some of the caked blood off Dan's hoof and dropped it into a plastic bag. He squinted up at me. "Cassie, I think you need to come work with us."

I blinked back at him. "I'm happy flying airplanes."

He looked at Frank. "You need to talk to her. She could be an asset to our operation."

Frank shrugged. "Cassie has her own ideas, and there's no way you or I are going to change her mind." He knelt beside the blood stains. "How does this change your theory of what happened?"

Greg closed the bag of scrapings and sat back on his heels. "How does this sound? The thieves got whatever they were after from Cassie's uncle, and one of them shot Charlie as they were leaving. The horse attacks and disables the guy we found. His buddy decides it's better to kill him than to try to take him along, so he shoots him and leaves."

"Wow," I said. "So much for honor among thieves."

"But it makes sense." Frank ran his hand through his hair. "Anything else?"

"We found a 9mm handgun next to the dead guy. Let's say my

theory is right. The guy you found here realizes his buddy is abandoning him and gets off his own shot first. That explains the blood you saw on the grass." He looked up at Frank. "By the way, did the hospital have a record of anybody coming in with a gunshot wound other than Cassie's uncle?"

"No. I checked with them when I got there." Frank rubbed the back of his neck. "Do you know what kind of gun killed the guy we found?"

"It was a .45 ACP," Greg said. "A lot bigger than a .9mm. We found the bullet lodged in the dirt."

They walked into the barn, and I followed them, holding on to Old Dan's halter. The hair on the back of my neck stood up. This was the general area where Uncle Charlie told me the secret was hidden. Unfortunately, he didn't tell me exactly what it was or precisely where he had hidden it, but he said it was around Dan's stall.

While Frank and Greg were conferring with each other in the middle of the barn, I put Dan back in his stall and walked around behind it. Nothing seemed to be disturbed there. Old Dan neighed softly at me as I looked through the tack box behind his stall, but there was nothing in it but scrapers, brushes, and hoof picks. I eased back into his stall, rubbed the old guy's nose, and scratched behind his ears.

Maybe it was inside the stall. I pretended to be looking for a brush while I walked around the stall, talking to Dan all the time. I looked inside his feed trough and between the slats in the sides. Nothing. Whatever it was, Uncle Charlie must have hidden it somewhere that wouldn't be obvious. Even to me.

"What are you looking for?" Frank's voice startled me as I was poking my fingers in between the boards on the stall.

"Just making sure everything's okay in here." I tried to look innocent, but when I faced him, his expression left no doubt. He didn't believe me. That's not surprising. I hate liars, and I've never wanted to mislead anybody, but now that's exactly what I was trying to do. I knew I wasn't convincing, but I had to honor my promise to Uncle Charlie.

"I was getting reacquainted with Dan," I said. "I used to ride this old guy when I came for a visit. He was my favorite of all of Uncle Charlie's horses." That part of what I was saying was the absolute truth.

"Too bad he can't talk," Frank said. "Maybe he could tell us some things." He held the door of the stall open for me to come out. "Seemed to me like you were looking for something in there. Maybe I should take a look." He stepped in, and I watched him check the same things I had. He didn't have any better luck.

He patted Old Dan's rump and walked out of the stall as Greg came back. "Let's go over to that little Mexican diner that's on the way to Bridgeton," he said. "We can talk over the situation while we eat."

Chapter 10

Sally's Salsa Cafe

Sally's Salsa Cafe was a culinary oasis planted in the middle of a sea of sand and mountains. It consisted of one small room of booths and tables, most of them filled with customers. Frank stayed outside to make a call while Greg and I moved in and found a table.

Greg pulled his hat off, exposing a head of wispy hair the color of strawberry ice cream. He dropped the baseball cap on the seat beside him and smoothed his mop.

The waitress placed glasses of water and menus in front of us. "I'll be back in a sec to take your orders," she said.

I gulped down the entire glass of water before I even glanced at the menu.

Greg tilted his head to one side and watched me drown my thirst. There was something about his light blue eyes and his steady gaze that made me think there was a lot going on inside his head. He grinned, which made the scar on his face stand out. "You must've been pretty dry."

"Like the Sahara," I said. "I didn't realize it until she brought the water."

He sipped from his own glass. "You need to stay hydrated, Cassie, especially in this heat."

"How do you do it?" I asked.

"We carry water around with us all the time."

"That's not what I meant. I mean, how do you look so normal when you're dealing with horrible people and murders? Doesn't that affect you psychologically?"

Greg sat back in the bentwood chair and nodded his head slowly. "I had a real hard time with it when I was in the field." His eyes focused on me. "I used to be Frank's partner when we both worked for the DEA."

"What was that like?"

"Frank's a dedicated man, a great partner. But the work is dangerous." He touched the scar on the side of his face. "After I had a little episode with a man waving a big knife, I decided I wasn't cut out for tracking down the bad guys and getting attacked, so I moved back here. Now I follow up on the forensics side of things."

We ordered our dinners and dug into the chips and salsa the waitress left with us.

"I thought Frank had another partner. Somebody named Jerry," I said.

Greg stuffed a tortilla chip in his mouth and swallowed. "Yeah. When I left DEA, Jerry came on board as Frank's partner. I only met Jerry once. He was real laid-back, and I figured he'd get himself killed. You know what happened when those drug kingpins lured him into a trap at Livingston Airport that day. After that, Jerry quit law enforcement altogether."

"Sounds like Frank has trouble keeping partners."

Greg shrugged. "So, tell me about yourself," he said between bites. "Is Cassie your real name?"

"It's a nickname. Short for Cassandra."

"Cassandra, eh?"

"Yeah. Cassandra is a character in Greek mythology. She was a mortal who was punished by the Greek gods and sentenced to always tell the truth."

"That doesn't sound like punishment to me," he said.

"The other part of the sentence is that no one ever believed her. She was the person who said 'Beware Greeks bearing gifts' about the Trojan horse. The Trojans didn't believe her, and you know what happened to them."

He gave me a big smile. "I'll believe everything you say, and I think the name Cassie suits you just fine."

We chomped on in silence for a few minutes. Between bites, Greg said, "Frank says you're the best pilot he's ever flown with."

I choked on a chip and had to take a few more swallows of water. "I can't believe Frank said that about me."

"He did. He told me all about that adventure at Livingston Airport."

I thought back to that day when Michael had ordered me to fly the stranger, Frank White, to another airport, but everything went haywire. "I just happened to have a can of red paint in the plane that I was taking to Uncle Charlie," I said. "It was one of those days where things seem to line up the right way and it all works out for the best." The exact opposite of today.

"Frank sure was impressed," Greg said.

I took another chip and made an effort to look interested in the napkin I was wiping my mouth with.

"He likes you," he said softly.

"I don't think so." I shrugged so Greg would get the point. "I think Frank's kind of stuck on himself. You should have seen him with that little candy-striper at the hospital today. He's probably outside calling her now, asking her to dinner."

The waitress came back with our orders, and I dove into the chimichanga with gusto. I figured that was a good way to avoid a conversation about a man I didn't want to talk about.

We ate in silence for a few minutes, and I was aware of Greg eyeing me as he chowed down on his tortilla. "Frank's reluctant to get into a serious relationship." He dropped that sentence out there in a low voice, but I visualized it in all caps, bolded, and italicized.

I put the chimichanga on my plate and tried to take another tack. "Sorry to hear about that," I said. "I just thought he didn't have a heart. You know, like he was more interested in other body parts."

Greg guffawed. "Maybe he just needs a good woman."

"Sure hope he finds her, but it's none of my business."

"I think it is," he said.

I sometimes wonder why people think they have to help me with relationships. My father used to tell me I was too focused on myself and I should open up to others. I just happen to be a very private person, and I'm obviously not a genius when it comes to men. I guess my standards are too high. They have to be able to read at a third-grade level. And they have to be honest. And trustworthy.

Greg put his second tortilla down and leaned forward. "I'm going to tell you something about Frank, but I don't want you to let him know I told you."

Just at that moment, Frank walked in and that was the end of our little private chat. As soon as Frank sat down, the waitress popped over and gave him a special smile. All Greg and I had gotten were the menus.

Chapter 11

Going Home

We all returned to the farm. Frank and I said our goodbyes to Greg and flew back to Bridgeton. The Bridgeton Airport is a small, general aviation operation. It's located within a mile of the hospital, so I made arrangements for Scout to be refueled, and we walked to the hospital.

When we got upstairs, I was surprised to see a uniformed officer outside Uncle Charlie's room. "Just being extra cautious," Frank said. He stayed outside to talk to the policeman while I slipped into the room.

Uncle Charlie was still sleeping peacefully, and the machines were bleeping and blinking in harmony. His face had more color than before, and that gave me a sense of peace. I sat next to his bed for an hour or so, holding his hand and talking to him about all the great things we'd do when he woke up. Then I said a prayer and thought about what I could do that would be the most help to him.

After I made up my mind, I grabbed my overnight bag and walked out into the hall. Mandy and Frank were standing next to her cart, talking in low tones. When she saw me, she gave him a little wave and pushed her cart down the hall. I guessed she and

Frank must be making arrangements for later, and I felt my face getting hot with the thought he was feathering his own bed while my uncle was lying injured.

"I'm going to fly back home," I said. "The nurse said Uncle Charlie won't wake up until tomorrow, so I'll come back in the morning with enough clothes that I can stay at the farm as long as he needs me."

"Good idea." Frank's voice was low, and he seemed distracted. Maybe he had Mandy on his mind. He looked up. "Will you be all right to fly? Not too upset?"

"I don't upset easily," I said as I walked toward the door.

He caught my arm as I was passing him. "Cassie," he said, "be careful. You never know who you can trust."

Now that was funny. Frank White advising me on the subject of trust. "I'll be fine," I said. Then I tossed my head and left.

* * *

I walked back to the airport where we had left Scout and did my pre-flight checks. Everything was perfect, and I felt the itch to get back in the sky.

When I got in the plane, I noticed a small canvas bag on the passenger seat. I opened it and found Frank's .38 pistol there. Why did he leave it for me? Maybe it was more of his law enforcement "everybody needs a gun" mindset. But as far as I was concerned, the danger was over.

I filed a flight plan and took off. As I climbed over the end of the runway, I looked back and saw a man standing in front of the hospital. From my distance and altitude, I couldn't see him well, but I was sure it was Frank.

It was late afternoon, my favorite time to fly. The earth was cooling down, the air was still, and my little plane slipped along as if it was riding on a silk thread. The trip back to Newton gave me time to think and process everything that had happened during the day.

In the middle of every thought stood Frank.

Frank made me uncomfortable. The way he smirked at me, like we were sharing some kind of private joke. A kind of flirtatious nothing-burger that handsome men are known for.

Not that I'm an authority. I'm twenty-five years old, and I haven't had many boyfriends. My father used to tell me I was too competitive. "A man wants a woman to come alongside him," he used to say. "Not somebody who's always competing with him."

Well, I can't turn myself into somebody else's idea of me. That would be wrong.

One of the gauges on an airplane's panel is called the Attitude Indicator. It shows a little outline of an airplane on a horizontal line. You can see if the plane is above or below the line, indicating it's climbing or descending. You can also tell if the plane is turning by the way the wings tilt in one direction or the other.

Ever since I met Frank, I've felt like my internal Attitude Indicator is all messed up. People have always called me levelheaded, but I wasn't level at all when I was around him. I felt like I was climbing, diving, and flying around in circles.

It's an awful situation to be fiercely attracted to someone you think you shouldn't have anything to do with. And I knew I was going to have to deal with Frank as long as there was an investigation into the attack on Uncle Charlie. I found myself sighing as Scout glided swiftly along.

Air traffic control broke into my thoughts. "Cessna Three One Four Bravo Charlie, you're approaching the Newton Airport."

I was glad for the interruption. I was back in my world where I felt comfortable and in charge. "Roger that." I spotted the lights of the runway. "I'd like to cancel flight-following at this time. I'll take it on in."

"Roger, Cessna Three One Four Bravo Charlie. Have a nice night."

I reset my transponder, flew the pattern, and set Scout down. I taxied over to the tarmac and parked my plane in its usual spot, tied it down, and carried my overnight bag into the office. Michael met me at the door.

Michael was the owner of the flight academy, and he was on site at all hours. I guessed he was probably working on the books. "I heard there was trouble," he said.

"Yeah. Some guys robbed my uncle's farm and shot him. He's doing okay, though."

"Sorry to hear it, Cassie, but I'm glad Frank was with you. I sure would've hated for you to fly into that mess by yourself."

I thought about that for a minute. What would have happened if Frank hadn't had that appointment with Uncle Charlie? My uncle could have lain there wounded for who knows how long. I shuddered and said a prayer of thanks.

"Michael, I may need to take some time off to take care of my uncle."

"No problem," he said. "Take all the time you need."

"Can you arrange for Scout to be refueled so I can fly back to the farm tomorrow morning?"

"Sure," he said. "I'll get the fuel truck over there now." He punched an icon on his phone.

I turned to leave, and Michael called out, "Be careful, Cassie."

What was it with everyone telling me to be careful? The danger was over, and I was going home to have a nice hot shower and get a good night's sleep. I threw my overnight bag into the back seat of my midnight blue Mustang and headed home.

* * *

I parked on the street and jogged toward the front door of the little house I bought the year after my dad passed away. I stood on the front porch, lost in thought about Uncle Charlie and Frank and Greg.

I was beginning to feel like Dorothy in *The Wizard of Oz*. I was part of a team that would have to figure out what happened to Uncle Charlie. The first team member, Greg, didn't have the courage to fight the bad guys, and the second one, Frank, didn't have the heart for building a relationship with a woman. Now all I needed was a third acquaintance. One without a brain.

I put the key in the front door and pushed it open.

My roommate was sitting on the couch, reading a copy of *Elle* and twirling a lock of long, blonde hair around her finger. She looked right at me when I walked in and called out, "Is that you?"

Meet my roommate, Dolly.

Chapter 12

Dolly

Dolores Isabella Raybourn is a cream puff with big, blonde hair, blue eyes surrounded by heavy, curled eyelashes, and a lack of anything approaching logic. And yet, in some incredible way, Dolly is an ideal roommate.

Dolly and I met just after my father died. She worked at the florist shop where many people ordered flowers for the funeral, and she had contacted me to ask if I wanted the green plants to be delivered to my home instead of the cemetery.

It was a kind gesture. I would never have thought about it, but when I stopped in the florist shop later to thank her in person, Dolly's obvious compassion for the families of people who had died impressed me.

We discovered we went to the same church but attended different services. I almost always go to the small Saturday night service since Sunday is often a busy day for me, while Dolly usually attends Sunday morning.

When I heard Dolly's apartment building was going to be demolished to make way for a parking lot and she was looking for a place to stay until she found another apartment, I offered her the guest room in my house. Heck, I didn't need all that room, and it was nice to see the lights on in the house when I came home from a flight.

And did I mention the fact that Dolly knows how to cook? How somebody who can't add two and two and get four can whip together a gourmet meal from a few leftovers and some canned goods is beyond me. But Dolly is a miracle in the kitchen.

We got along well, and after a couple of months, it didn't seem to make any sense for her to have to move again. So she pays me a little rent every month, and I eat decently. She and I agreed on the rules, and things worked out fine.

The other talent Dolly has is an overabundance of common sense. She may not know who the second president of the United States was, but she can talk to a young girl who just lost her mother and make her understand that her life will go on.

Dolly put the magazine on the table and swung her magnificently pedicured feet into the fluffy sunshine-yellow bedroom slippers on the floor.

"So, how was your day?" she asked. "I thought you said you were going to be back from your trip earlier."

Since my trips are often delayed by weather or changes in plans, Dolly and I agreed she should never wait for me. If she cooks enough for two, I can always eat leftovers.

"Something terrible happened, Dolly." I dropped the overnight bag on the floor and sank into one of the easy chairs facing her. "Uncle Charlie's been shot."

"Oh, no!" Dolly's hand covered her heart.

"He's going to be okay, but he's in the hospital at Bridgeton. That's the little town close to his farm. I just wanted to come home so I could shower and pick up some clothes to go back to the hospital tomorrow morning."

"You look exhausted, poor thing."

"I'll be okay after a good night's sleep."

"Well, I made a chicken casserole for dinner, and there's plenty left over. I'll warm it up for you."

"Thanks." I hauled myself up out of the chair and started toward my bedroom, but I stopped after a couple of steps and turned back. "Dolly, can I ask you a personal question?"

"Sure," she said as she neatly adjusted the magazines on the coffee table.

"Do you use an eyelash curler?"

She looked up and raised her eyebrows. "Of course. Everybody does. It's just a part of being a woman."

I clomped back to my bedroom. My mother died when I was just a baby. My dad raised me by himself, and he was a good father, but it dawned on me now that I had missed a lot by not having a woman around when I was growing up.

I pulled clean clothes from my chest of drawers and turned the shower on full blast. While the water heated up, I stared at my reflection in the bathroom mirror. "Too late, Cassie," I said out loud. "You are what you are."

I stepped into the shower and replayed the day's events in my mind as the hot water washed over me. Once again, Frank was in the middle of every scene. Frank holding me back from running into the house. Frank's arm around me while Uncle Charlie was loaded into the ambulance. Frank searching the area for clues as if he knew the farm as well as I did.

And what was it that Greg wanted to tell me? He said there was something about Frank I should know, but we got interrupted before he shared that bit of wisdom.

I turned the water off and towel-dried my hair. Something was tapping at my brain, telling me to think it through. I was missing something.

I pulled on my clothes and finished drying my hair. When I left my room, I was met by Fiddlesticks, Dolly's condescending Siamese cat. Fiddlesticks has come to the conclusion that she owns my house, and she finds my presence so annoying that she retreats to Dolly's room whenever I'm around. I've never seen her even stoop to put one of her dainty little paws into my bedroom. No problem there. I'm not much of a cat person anyway.

However, having a cat turns out to be a pretty good idea. My little house is part of a subdivision that was developed on land that had once been a farm. Some of my neighbors have complained about field mice, but we've never seen any. I suspect Fiddlesticks is good at guarding against unwelcome guests, so I'm okay with her sticking her nose up in the air and strutting around like the queen.

I didn't realize I was hungry again until the aroma from the kitchen drew me in. Do people always eat this much when they've experienced trauma?

Dolly's mother was Jewish, so Dolly always lights candles on Friday evening and calls our meal Shabbat Dinner. She was fussing with a hot casserole and green salad when I came in. "Sit down," she called over her shoulder. "I want to hear what happened."

I looked carefully at Dolly's profile as she spooned out the meal onto my plate. She's at least thirty years old, but she looks much younger. I'm twenty-five, and Dolly doesn't look any older than I do. Maybe I can learn some things from her.

Between bites of a fabulous casserole that must have been thousands of calories, I filled her in on what had happened that day. Dolly is a good listener. It's nice to have a friend to spill your insides to. I told her I had decided to help the police in their investigation.

"What?" Her eyes got about as big as the dinner plate I was eating from. "Cassie, are you crazy? That's dangerous." One thing about Dolly. She can spot the obvious.

"Yes, I know. But we're talking about Uncle Charlie. Somebody took a shot at him. He could have been killed." I gulped down a swallow of water. "I want to know who did it and why. It's not about revenge, Dolly. It's about justice."

Dolly gripped the edge of the table. "You could get yourself killed."

Another common sense bit of the undeniable. And I had to admit she was right. I'm Cassie Deakin, one of the members of a family that has always had trouble maneuvering through a 24-hour day without spilling coffee in their laps or twisting an ankle just walking down the street. We're great at driving a car, riding a horse, or flying an airplane, but definitely challenged on the ground. I'd probably be more dangerous to the police than the criminals.

Still, I'm pretty smart. I'm an excellent pilot, and even Frank said how creative I was when I saved him from that band of drug lords a couple of months ago.

I can do a lot of things. Just as long as I don't have to walk down a runway in high heels, I'll be fine.

Chapter 13

Return to the Hospital

After Dolly and Fiddlesticks went to bed, I packed a week's worth of clothes into a large duffel bag and placed it by the front door. Then I set the coffeemaker for five a.m. and made sure there was cereal so I could grab breakfast and get to the airport by six.

I pulled on my pajamas and crawled into bed, hoping to get a few hours of rest, but all I did was flop around. There was something bothering me, tugging at my brain cells, but I couldn't figure out what it was. I heard the clock in the living room strike midnight, and I was still wide awake.

The day had been like running a marathon. While you're in the middle of it, you can't see the whole picture, but afterward, you look back and notice the little things you hadn't thought of during the race. I tried to do that as I lay on my back. What had I missed?

Then I remembered. When we discovered Uncle Charlie had been shot, Frank said, "I'm going to check the toolshed." But how did he know about the toolshed? That was the first time he'd been to Uncle Charlie's place. He was asleep when I landed the plane, so he couldn't have seen it from the air, and he didn't see it when we walked out to the barn. It was on the other side of the building.

I sat up in bed. Did Frank know more than he let on? Why would he keep anything from me?

And then there was something about the hospital that was a little off. The doctors and nurses were efficient and helpful, but I saw Nurse Ratched exchange a glance with the doctor that looked like there was a message in it. And what about the candy-striper? Mandy. She seemed to be everywhere.

My dad used to say I could get tunnel vision when I locked onto a problem. Every thought pushed me into thinking there was something wrong at the hospital. And my uncle was lying unconscious there.

I reached for my phone. My breath quickened. Should I call the hospital? Or Frank? My dad's words came back to me. "Be careful who you put your trust in."

Whom could I trust? The answer flashed in my mind like a big neon sign. Nobody.

I swung my legs over the side of the bed and got dressed. The digital clock on my nightstand blinked out the time. Twelve-thirty. But the adrenaline was pumping, and I knew I wouldn't sleep until I was sure Uncle Charlie was safe. I wrote a note to Dolly explaining that I had to go back to the hospital, and then I quietly hoisted the duffel bag onto my shoulder and hurried to my car.

Fortunately for me, Newton Airport has a lighted runway, and someone mans the tower at all hours. The planes were lined up on the tarmac like toys sitting on a shelf, just waiting to be taken out and flown. Scout had already been refueled, and I ran through my checklist.

On any other night, I would have stopped to admire the crescent moon and a spray of glittering stars. But on this night, I only wanted to get back to the hospital and convince myself that Uncle Charlie was alive.

Normally, it wouldn't be wise to fly in the middle of the night after such a harrowing day. But I wasn't tired. Just the opposite. I was hyper-alert.

I called in the flight plan. No use going off into a dark night without making sure air traffic control was following. I keyed the ignition, and Scout responded like a dream. My mind turned to the task at hand, and after the run-up and clearance, I lifted off the runway into a cloudless sky.

Nighttime flying is like entering another world. In this part of the country, there are just a few lights on the ground, so from five thousand feet above ground level, it's as if you're navigating alone in the universe, drifting under a black canopy punctuated by stars.

I was heading west toward the constellation Ursa Major. I said a silent prayer of thanks for the calm air and clear sky, but even the serenity of flight couldn't ease my mind.

There's no tower at the small airport in Bridgeton, but I keyed a sequence on my yoke that illuminated the runway lights so I could land. I set Scout down and pulled over into the tie-down area. Mr. Olson came walking out of the office.

"I didn't expect to see you back here, young lady," he said as he helped me secure the wings and tail of my plane.

"I was worried about my uncle and decided to come back to check on him," I said. "I can walk to the hospital from here."

"You don't need to walk. I'll drive you over."

"That would be fantastic. Thank you." I grabbed my duffel bag from the back seat of the plane and juggled my purse to the other arm.

"Here, give me that." He took the duffel bag from me, and I felt a rush of appreciation for this wiry old guy who had spent his life in aviation. He could probably fly rings around the rest of us, but he served his community by manning the nighttime office of a small airport.

I paid him the fee for the tie-down and asked to have Scout refueled. He locked the office, and we drove to the hospital in silence.

He dropped me off in the front area and tipped his hat good-bye. As I watched him drive away, I had that same sensation that I had earlier. A feeling that something was out of focus. Like I wasn't seeing clearly with my mind's eye. I wondered if I was suffering some kind of PTSD, but whatever it was would have to wait until I got to Uncle Charlie's room. I swung the duffel bag over my shoulder and hurried toward the door.

The on-duty policeman at the front door yawned and asked for my ID. I fished around in my purse and handed him my driver's license. They were just changing shifts, and the officer coming on duty frowned at me. "Let me see that ID," he said in a voice that sounded like he had gargled with sandpaper. He made a big deal out of checking my picture and handed the license back to me. I didn't like his attitude, but, on the other hand, it made me feel good that they were being extra careful.

I signed in and walked up the stairs to the second floor. When I came out of the stairwell, I saw the uniformed policeman sitting in the hallway next to the door to my uncle's room. He recognized me from earlier in the day. "Couldn't stay away?" he asked.

"I feel better being here," I said. He nodded in understanding and held the door for me to go in.

The room was dark, but the monitors were chirping out an optimistic tune, and I could make out the big lump of Uncle Charlie in the hospital bed, snoring quietly.

I dropped my bag on the floor next to the bed and watched Uncle Charlie breathing in, breathing out. Everything appeared normal and secure.

I decided I had overreacted. I do have a tendency to get super-focused on one or two details and lose perspective of the big picture. And things always look bleak in the middle of the night, I told myself, and felt the sense of dread lift off my shoulders.

In my rush to return, I hadn't brought any water with me, so I stepped into the hall to look for a vending machine. Everything was quiet. I asked the policeman if he knew where I could get a bottle of water, and he pointed down the hall to the left. As I turned, I saw the new policeman from downstairs come out of the stairwell door. I was grateful to know he took his job seriously. He looked around furtively and lifted his gun out of its holster. I was just getting ready to wave when a voice from the other end of the hall behind me, shouted. "Hit the floor! He has a gun."

I've heard that there are times when your body reacts to something even before your brain tells it to. This must have been one of those times because my legs collapsed under me. Before I could even decipher what was said, I was flat on the floor, and I heard a bullet whiz over my head. The policeman at the end of the hall fell, and I saw a spreading stain of blood form around him. I looked back to see where the shot had come from.

There, standing at the other end of the hall and holding a Glock, stood candy-striper Mandy.

Chapter 14

The Policeman

The policeman who had been stationed outside Uncle Charlie's room jumped over me and raced down the hall. Mandy started to run toward me. I pushed backward into Uncle Charlie's room and shoved the door shut with my foot.

I sat there on the floor, hearing the rasping noise of my own breath and trying to make sense of what was going on. Whatever it was, my job was to protect Uncle Charlie. I held the door closed with my foot and looked wildly around the room for a weapon. I thought about the canvas bag sitting on the passenger seat of my plane. Why didn't I keep the gun Frank gave me? I could at least defend myself and Uncle Charlie, but I was isolated and unarmed.

I looked back at Uncle Charlie. He was still snoring, drugged into the sleep of the innocent. I scanned the room for something I could use as a weapon. Anything.

There was a loud *thump-thump* of shoes running in the hall and voices shouting. Then someone pushed against the door. There are no locks on the hospital doors. I held my foot fast, but I knew I wasn't a match for the person on the other side trying to muscle their way in.

"Cassie! Cassie, are you all right?" It was Frank's voice.

I bit my lip. At that moment, I felt more alone than I ever had. I was in a world of strangers. The only person I knew I could trust was lying in the bed behind me, and I wasn't going to let anyone else in until I could figure out what was going on.

"Cassie, let me in!" The door moved.

"No!" I shouted.

There was silence on the other side of the door. Then Frank's voice came through, calm and quiet. "Cassie, it's me, Frank. You're not in any danger. Let me in."

The door slowly moved toward me and there was no way my foot could prevent him from opening it. I jumped up and ran next to Uncle Charlie's bed.

The door pushed all the way open and Frank stood in the doorway. With the light behind him, I couldn't see the expression on his face. He was just the silhouette of a man holding a gun.

I stood next to the bed with my arms spread wide, as if that would protect my beloved uncle.

My world was officially out of control. The only thing I could think of was to try to act like I was in command of the situation. I clenched my fists until my fingernails dug into the palms of my hands. "Go away and leave us alone," I demanded and willed my face into a mask of authority.

Frank shoved his gun into the shoulder holster as he walked toward me. "Cassie, you know I wouldn't hurt you or your uncle. If I wanted to do him harm, I had all day to do it."

Of course, he was right. He could have killed Uncle Charlie while I was away. My brain reeled. None of it made any sense. I turned my back to him.

I'm not a panicky person. I once landed an airplane in a farmer's cornfield when the engine quit during a sudden storm. It wasn't easy, but I knew exactly what I had to do. I had trained for it. It took all my concentration and skill, and I put the plane on the ground safely.

But this was different. Nothing had prepared me for this. My job was to protect Uncle Charlie, but I didn't know how. I held onto the railing of the bed to stop my hands from shaking. A torrent of fear and fury bubbled up from inside me, and I tasted the salty tears as they ran down my face.

Frank came up behind me, put his hands on my shoulders, and turned me toward him. His face had lost all its usual cool, and he was just a man comforting a frightened woman.

He pulled me to him and held me firmly. He kept repeating, "It's okay. It's okay," as he rubbed my back. "Michelle just shot a man who was impersonating an officer. He might have harmed your uncle, but he's not going to hurt anybody now."

I didn't understand what he was talking about. My brain resembled an old lava lamp with blobs of thought moving around randomly but not getting anywhere.

I clung to him, not knowing if he was a good guy or if he was just impersonating a good guy. Whatever he was, he was there.

He gently set me down in the chair next to the bed and knelt beside me, stroking my hair as I put my head in my hands. I don't know how long I sat there or what I would see when I looked up. What did he say? He said Michelle shot somebody.

"Who is Michelle?" I asked between hiccups.

"Michelle is a police detective who was undercover as a candy-striper in order to stay close to your uncle."

"Michelle is Mandy?" I felt my eyes turning into saucers and wiped them with my hands.

"Right. It's a little hard to explain, but I guess I'm going to have to let you in on it now." Frank grabbed a handful of tissues from the night table and handed them to me. "You should wipe your nose."

While I was trying to clean up and stop shaking, Mandy walked into the room. "Are you okay?" she asked.

I turned in the chair to look at her. She was still holding her Glock down by her side, and the flirty, girly expression that she wore earlier in the day was gone. "Who *are* you?" I shouted. "Why are you dressed like that and firing off a gun in a hospital?"

"We'll explain it to you when you calm down," Frank said. "We didn't think you were coming back to the hospital tonight. You told me you'd come back in the morning. You could have been hurt."

"No kidding. Walking around this hospital is downright dangerous, especially with people like her." I pointed at Mandy or Michelle or whoever she was.

Chapter 15

Undercover

Frank took my arm and guided me out of the room. As we exited, I saw a team of men, including Greg, bending over the alleged policeman who was lying on the floor at the end of the hall.

Greg stood and made a thumbs-down motion.

"What does that mean?" I asked, but it was obvious what he was saying. Frank didn't even bother to answer.

He led me to a room at the other end of the hall. A couple of cots had been set up, and there were several laptops sitting on those tables that normally have hospital food on them.

"Stay here," Frank said. "I'll be right back." He left Mandy/Michelle and me alone.

I sat in a chair facing her and tried to be civil, but my natural talent for sarcasm popped out. "Do you go around impersonating an innocent candy-striper at all the hospitals? Or is this a special occasion?"

She chuckled. "I can understand your confusion, Cassie, but I think you're reading the situation wrong." She took out her badge and showed it to me. I noticed she wasn't wearing a wedding ring, but her hand was pale around the third finger on her left hand.

She caught me looking. "I didn't wear my wedding ring because I'm undercover here." She laughed. "It's the first time I've had an assignment that called for me to act like a single girl on the prowl. What did you think of my performance?"

"Very realistic," I huffed out.

She arched an eyebrow. "Don't worry. I'm happily married with a great husband and two kids. I'm not competition for you."

"I have no idea what you mean."

"I think you do," she said. "You know, he ..."

She was interrupted when Frank strode back into the room. "Did I miss anything?"

"No," I said with as much emphasis as I could add. "I want to know what's going on."

Frank pulled a chair up next to me. "Cassie, I was sent to interview your uncle because Ruddy thought he might have some information about a death that happened forty years ago."

"Forty years ago? That would have been ..." I paused, trying to do the math.

"1970," Frank said.

"What information could Uncle Charlie possibly have?"

"Someone phoned Ruddy a week or so ago and said he wanted an investigation re-opened about a death that happened in 1970 that was ruled an accident. He said he believed it was a murder, and your uncle was in possession of some information that could be important. Ruddy didn't think there was much to it, but he assigned me to the case. I talked to your uncle on the phone and set up the interview."

I faced him and pointed a finger right in his face. "How did you know about the toolshed?"

"What?"

"The toolshed. You said you were going to check the toolshed when we were in the barn, but there's no way you could have known about it."

The edges of Frank's mouth turned up, and he shook his head. "You really are something."

"That's what people say." I stuck my bottom lip out. "Answer the question. How did you know about the toolshed?"

"When I set up the interview, your uncle told me he was repairing the toolshed behind the barn."

"Oh." I sucked my lip back in and bit it.

"Is that why you came back to the hospital tonight? Because you thought I was hiding something?"

"You're a very suspicious-looking person," I said and humphed to put a fine point on it.

Frank's grin disappeared. "People are not always what they seem to be," he said. "I'm glad you were skeptical. It means you won't be easily misled."

I filed that statement away inside my head which was throbbing with a terrible tear-drained headache. "Why didn't you tell me you'd already talked to Uncle Charlie?"

"That should be obvious, Cassie. We don't include people who might be put in danger by the knowledge."

"That policeman. Was he here to hurt Uncle Charlie?"

"I'm afraid so. It's not unusual for an assassin to impersonate a police officer, and when one of our men saw him coming into the building, he alerted Michelle who took care of the situation. You just happened to be in the wrong place at the wrong time."

"It's one of my special talents."

His eyes sparkled, and the lines around them deepened in amusement. "Michelle said you have quick reflexes."

"I guess that comes in handy around here."

Something clicked inside of me. Uncle Charlie's life had been put in danger not once, but twice, and I realized I couldn't just keep floating through this situation, saying I was going to help the police while depending on them to keep him safe. I had crossed a line. The one that stands between a person and what's wrong with the world. The line that says: From now on, I will take one hundred percent responsibility for this situation.

But I was still not sure about the people around me. Frank, Greg, Michelle. I feigned a yawn and said, "I want to know more, but right now I need to get some sleep. I'm going back to Uncle Charlie's room and get some shut-eye in the chair." I needed time to think.

Frank stood and took my arm. "I'll walk you home."

We moved out into the hall that was still crawling with police. I was hoping they were the real deal. When we reached Uncle Charlie's room, Frank opened the door for me and followed me in.

"Thanks," I said.

"Anytime." He closed the door behind us and turned back to me.

It was dark and quiet in the room. I could barely make out Frank's eyes fixed on me. He put his hands on my shoulders, and I felt his warm breath on my face as he pulled me to him. I didn't resist. His kiss wasn't a peck on the cheek or a sloppy goodnight kiss. It was deep and passionate, and I felt my knees go weak.

He released me, and we stood in silence for a few seconds. Then he turned and left.

And they say women are hard to understand.

Chapter 16

A New Day

I waited until I got my equilibrium back before I moved. I had never been kissed like that before, and I sensed there was some unfulfilled need in Frank that I had just been drawn into. Whatever it was, it would have to wait.

I shook my head and walked shakily across the room. This was not the time for romantic complications. I had to put Frank out of my mind and concentrate on my job. I moved the hospital chair so it was between Uncle Charlie's bed and the door. If anybody came in during the night, they'd have to climb over me to get to him.

I spent some quality time thinking as I sat in that chair, and I fell asleep considering the situation. Whatever Uncle Charlie had gotten himself involved in, I was in it too, and I wasn't going to sit around waiting for some gangster types to hurt me or my uncle.

I woke up with a stiff neck and a sore back when Nurse Ratched showed up around six o'clock to check all Uncle Charlie's vital signs. Gone was the clipped and bureaucratic manner she had intimidated me with the day before. She stood in front of me with her hands on her hips. "Are you all right?" she asked in a surprisingly soft voice.

I blinked a couple of times to be sure this was the same woman. "Yes, I'm fine. Just a little stiff." I stood and stretched.

"I heard what happened last night."

I stopped my stretching and faced her. "Are you one of them?" I asked. "One of the undercover bunch?"

She actually smiled, showing a beautiful set of white teeth and some laugh lines around her mouth and eyes. That was comforting. "No. I just work here. But lately, we've been seeing some patients with gunshot wounds, and the police have been active in working with the hospital in case someone shows up to try to finish the job. I guess that happened last night."

She reviewed the blinking lights, changed the IV bag, and seemed satisfied that all was in order. "I'll be on duty all day today. Feel free to come get me if you need me." When she got to the door, she turned back. "I had a favorite uncle once. If anybody had threatened him ... well, I guess I know how you feel." She nodded at me and left.

After I washed my face and brushed my teeth in the little bathroom, I returned to the side of the bed and stood looking at the man who had taught me to ride horses and play poker. "I won't let you down," I whispered as if he could hear me.

There was a soft rap at the door and Frank came in. He had dark circles under his eyes, looking like he hadn't slept at all. "Hey," he said and moved over next to me. There was something different about him, something soft and kind around his eyes that wasn't there before. After that brief moment of passion last night, I wasn't sure how to act.

"Any change?" he asked.

I wanted to tell him that I intended to find out who had done this awful thing, but just then Uncle Charlie groaned. His eyes blinked and slowly opened. He stared at me, then at Frank, then back at me.

I had the terrifying thought that the concussion may have

messed with his brain and he wouldn't recognize me. "Uncle Charlie," I said, "it's me. It's Cassie."

My wonderful, funny, lovable, clumsy uncle frowned. "Of course it's you, Cassie. Don't you think I know my own niece?"

I laughed with tears in my eyes. "Oh, Uncle Charlie. It's so good to hear your voice!"

"What's all this?" He looked around at the various tubes and wires that were attached to him. "Where am I?"

"You're in the hospital. You had a gunshot wound and lost a lot of blood. How do you feel?"

"Like I've been shot and lost a lot of blood," he replied and smiled weakly. Then he looked over my shoulder. "Who's your young fella?"

"He's not my young fella."

Frank reached over and patted Uncle Charlie's hand. "I'm Frank White, sir. I was the one who called to set up the interview with you. It's good to see you awake."

Uncle Charlie blinked a couple of times. "I'm a little fuzzy on what's going on."

"Do you remember anybody causing trouble at your farm?" Frank asked.

Uncle Charlie groaned. "Oh yeah. I remember now. That scum face tried to shoot me." He squirmed a little. "I guess he hit the target. What's the story? Do I still have all my parts?"

Frank smiled. "Yep. I guess you're a pretty tough guy. The doctors said you lost a lot of blood, but you came through the operation with flying colors." He put his hand on my shoulder. "I think you owe a few pints of blood to your niece."

"How's my little sweetheart?" Uncle Charlie said and took my hand. "Did old Uncle Charlie give you a scare?"

I patted his hand. No reason to make him upset. "Uncle Charlie, I don't understand what's going on. All I know is that you're safe now and I intend to keep it that way."

He laughed. "My little Cassie. Look at that fiery expression on your face. I swear you're going to burn a hole right through my bandages."

"Uncle Charlie, you shouldn't be talking. The doctors said to let them know as soon as you woke up." I turned to Frank. "Would you mind telling the nurses that Uncle Charlie's awake? I'll just stay here."

After Frank was safely out of the room, I leaned closer to Uncle Charlie. "I looked for our secret, but you never told me exactly where you hid it. Is that what the thieves were after?"

Before he had a chance to answer, Frank returned with two nurses and a doctor.

Dr. Dudley looked surprised that his patient seemed alert. "What have we here?" he asked. I could tell by the wide smile on his face that he was happy to see the recovery.

"Hello, doc," Uncle Charlie replied. "When can I go home?"

Dr. Dudley laughed and looked at the data on a screen the nurse had rolled into the room. "Well, Mr. Deakin, it looks like you're making a remarkable recovery," he said. "We'll see how you feel in the morning, and we'll go from there."

They fussed around him, checking numbers and fluid levels. One of the nurses took his temperature and blood pressure while Frank and I stood at the foot of the bed feeling useless.

I followed the doctor out into the hall. "How long will he have to stay here?" I asked.

"We'll keep him for another day or two. Just depends on how quickly he responds to the medications." He looked back toward the room. "I saw on his chart that he's sixty-two years old, and I can see he's a vigorous man. I believe we'll be able to discharge him tomorrow or the next day."

"He'll be miserable here."

"Yes, I know. The strong ones don't adapt well to hospital life. Just try to keep him calm. It will help with the healing."

When I got back to the room, Frank was standing on the other side of the bed and talking in low tones.

"Am I interrupting an important conversation?" I was irritated that Frank decided to ask his questions before I even got back in the room.

"Come on in, honey," Uncle Charlie said cheerfully. "I was just shootin' the breeze with your young fella."

"He's not my young fella, Uncle Charlie, but he might be able to help us figure out what's going on."

"I sure hope so. Those young punks were up to no good."

Frank took a notebook out of his shirt pocket. "Do you feel up to telling us what happened?"

Chapter 17

The Robbery

Uncle Charlie adjusted the sheet. "I heard the motorcycle when they pulled up outside the house while I was eating breakfast. Must have been around seven o'clock or so. I thought it might be a couple of those bikers Cassie had introduced me to a few weeks ago. Maybe they knew she was flying over and wanted to say hello. I didn't think much of it, and I went out to the front porch to meet them."

"How many were there?" Frank asked.

"Two men riding on a big cycle. I don't know much about motorcycles. I guess it was a Harley."

"Did you recognize them?"

"No. They took off their helmets and came up on the porch. They seemed real polite. Said they were running short on hay for their horses and some folks in town told them I had hay for sale."

"Can you describe them?" Frank asked.

"They were like opposites. One tall and muscular. He wore a bandana on his head and had a scruffy look, like he hadn't shaved for a few days. The other one was short and slim. He was clean-shaven and his hair was sandy colored. He had on a clean T-shirt and jeans."

"What happened next?"

Uncle Charlie's eyes focused on the far wall. "I asked them how they planned to move the hay on that motorcycle, and they said they'd come back for it with a truck. They wanted to see it so we walked around the house back to the barn."

"Go on."

"We got to the barn, and I showed them the bales I had stacked on one side. I had about ten bales I was willing to sell. The short one lingered around the horse stalls. He said he loved horses, and he was asking me about them. Cassie'll tell you, I can talk a blue streak about my horses, and before you know it, I was telling him all about each one of them. When we got to Dan's stall, I was in high form, telling him all about how Dan was like a good friend. And that short guy seemed to be enjoying it all, smiling and laughing, and all the time turning me away from the other one."

Uncle Charlie shifted in the bed and I saw his mouth turn down at the corners. "I hate dishonest people," he said, almost to himself. "A man wants something—he should have the guts to say it to your face, not dance around a lie."

Frank glanced up at me. Honesty was the bedrock on which Uncle Charlie had built his life. He was born with a noble spirit, and he did not understand people who tried to cheat their way to an advantage in life.

Uncle Charlie's right hand fumbled with the sheet. "That's the reason I bought the farm," he said softly. "People in this part of the country are different. It's not an easy life out here. There's no room for playing games with each other. You take care of your animals and your farm, and that doesn't leave any time for highfalutin nonsense." He sighed and blinked hard. "I guess things are changing."

"That's for sure," Frank said. "I'm sorry to make you go through this, Charlie, but we need to know everything that happened."

"I finished telling Shorty about how great Dan was, and then I heard the other guy say, 'Turn around.' I did, and he was holding a gun on me."

His fist closed around the sheet. "The short guy told me to move away from Dan's stall. While I was trying to figure out how to get that gun away from Scruffy, the short one opened the door to Dan's stall and led him out. He tied Dan to the post outside his stall, and that's when I realized what was going on. He was searching for Sinclair's box."

"Whoa," Frank said. "What's Sinclair's box?"

Uncle Charlie and I exchanged a look, and Frank saw it.

"Cassie," Frank said. "Did you know about this box?"

I shuffled my feet and tried to look innocent. "Um, sort of," I said.

Frank's face turned dark. "You were withholding information."

"Now don't go blaming her," Uncle Charlie said and reached over to take my hand. "I told her a few days ago that I had hidden a box inside the barn and made her promise not to tell anyone. I wanted her to know in case anything happened to me. She was just keeping her promise." He looked at me and squeezed my hand. "It's no use keeping the promise now," he said. "It's gone."

"They took it?"

"Yep. They knew exactly what they were looking for, and approximately where to find it."

"Even I didn't know that," I said. "I looked all over Dan's stall, but I couldn't find it."

"It was in the false bottom of the tack box behind the stall."

"Ah. I didn't realize there was a false bottom."

"Okay. Keep going. What happened next?" Frank's pen was poised above the notebook.

"Shorty looked around inside the stall but didn't find anything. Then he walked behind the stall. He came out holding the box and handed it to the other guy. The big guy kept his gun trained on me the whole time, but then he turned to Shorty and said, 'Do it.' That's when Shorty pulled a gun on me and Big Guy walked out."

"Let me get this straight," Frank said. "You were left in the barn with the short one."

"Yeah. The little guy was sweating. I figured he hadn't killed anybody before, and I was his price of admission to a gang.

"All this time, Dan was pulling at the lead line that was tied around the post. He hates being tied up. Never could get him to behave. Shorty hadn't done much of a job with the lead line, and all of a sudden, Dan pulled loose and started toward Shorty."

Uncle Charlie's eyes lit up. "I sure wouldn't want to be the one Dan gets mad at," he said with a sharp chuckle. "I guess Shorty was thrown off balance when Dan charged him, so I thought that was my chance. I lunged toward the gun. That's when he shot me. It threw me back against the side of the stall and I went down.

"I remember hitting my head hard on something—probably the cement block that was lying on the ground. I saw stars, but I was still conscious.

"Dan reared, and Shorty jumped up and started to run, but Dan caught him just as he got to the door. The last thing I saw was Dan stomping that poor young punk." Uncle blinked hard and looked over at Frank. "He must have messed him up pretty bad."

"Yeah, he did," Frank said. "Do you remember anything else?"

"I heard a couple of gunshots and wondered if I'd been shot again. I was on the verge of passing out and figured I was a goner. The next thing I knew was when I saw Cassie kneeling beside me. I wanted to tell her to run, but I couldn't make my mouth work."

I shuddered, thinking of that moment.

"Let's get back to Sinclair." Frank was scribbling as he talked. "Who was he?"

Chapter 18

Sinclair

"Sinclair Alderson," Uncle Charlie said. "He was my closest friend in Vietnam." Uncle's eyes grew soft. "He saved my life."

"Sinclair saved your life?" Frank asked.

"Yes, he did." Uncle Charlie asked for water, and I handed him the cup that was on the night table. He took a sip and lay back on the pillow. "In one skirmish, we were ambushed by the Vietcong, and I took a shot in the leg." I remembered how he always favored his right leg a little when he walked. "I thought it was over for me, but Sinclair dragged me into a ditch and started firing like a crazy man. It was enough to hold off the Vietcong until a chopper could get to us." He glanced at me. "If Sinclair hadn't been there, your old Uncle Charlie's bones would be lying in the jungle right now."

"I didn't know any of this," I said. I had a horrible image of Uncle Charlie lying dead.

"It's not the kind of thing you talk about," he said. "All I wanted to do was forget that war and start my life over." He handed me the cup, and I put it back on the nightstand.

"Tell us more about Sinclair and how he figures into all this." Frank poised his hand to start writing again.

"When we were in Vietnam, Sinclair used to tell me about his little sister. Her name was Lacey, and he said she was the only good thing about his family. He said she was just a little kid—seven or eight years old—and she had some kind of learning disability which meant she couldn't learn things the way the rest of us do, but Sinclair said she was special. He was real fond of her and wanted me to meet her after we got discharged."

He gripped the sheet with his hand, and his eyelids drooped. "When we got back to the States, we thought we'd be welcomed as heroes, but when we got off the plane in Virginia, there was a crowd there booing us. Like we were traitors. I felt sick."

He got quiet, and I could see him reliving the disgrace of his homecoming. "That was before you were even born, Cassie."

"I'm sorry that happened to you," I said and touched his arm.

He turned his face to me and patted my hand. "It changed me, Cassie. All I wanted to do was get out of that place, so Sinclair and I headed west. He said I could meet his family, and he'd help me find a place to live out west. We changed into civilian clothes as quick as we could and took off. When we got to his parents' house, Sinclair got the shock of his life. Worse than Vietnam."

"What could be worse than that?" I asked.

"The house was empty. Nobody there. We went to a neighbor's house. A couple of spinsters a mile or two away. They said Lacey had died in an accident and Sinclair's parents had moved away." He shook his head. "Sinclair's parents didn't even write to tell him about Lacey's death. It was unforgivable.

"We talked to the sheriff in those parts, and he drove us to the place where Lacey fell down the side of a cliff. He said she must have been playing in the forest and slipped on some gravel and went over the side. It was a sheer drop down to a river. He showed us where they found one of her shoes and that's how they knew where she fell." Uncle took a deep breath.

"Are you tired, Uncle Charlie? Do you want to rest a while?" I asked.

"No, honey. I'm glad to talk about it. It's been forty years, but I never told anybody about Sinclair's sister before."

I held the cup of water for him. He took another sip and continued. "The sheriff said the body washed down the river and was discovered in Willard County, the next county over. He told us the sheriff there was in charge of the investigation, so we drove over.

"The Willard County sheriff was very nice and seemed concerned about Sinclair. He pulled out the file and showed us all the data about where she fell and where her body was found. He explained that she hadn't been assaulted in any way, and they felt sure she was probably unconscious when she hit the river, so she didn't really suffer."

"So Sinclair was comforted?"

"Not at all. He told the sheriff he was sure Lacey hadn't fallen off that cliff."

"How could he be sure?" Frank asked. "He was in Vietnam when it happened."

"Sinclair said Lacey was terrified of heights. He knew exactly where that cliff was and he even remembered being there once with Lacey when she pulled him away from the edge. He said Lacey got very agitated and yelled, 'Danger! Danger!' until he moved away from the edge."

"People change," I said. "Maybe Lacey decided to be brave and go to the edge of the cliff."

"That's exactly what I told Sinclair, but he was adamant. Lacey would not go near the cliff. He asked the sheriff to reopen the investigation. The sheriff said he'd personally look into it, but he told Sinclair he doubted there'd be enough evidence to warrant another look.

"When Sinclair stormed out, the sheriff told me it happens a lot with accident victims. Their family can't believe it wasn't foul play."

"Did Sinclair ever find anything to back up his claim?" Frank asked.

"No. He knew he couldn't prove anything. We went back to his parents' house. Really, it was more of a shack. He found a little box with some of Lacey's things. He loaded those in his car and told me he couldn't stay anywhere near that place, and he headed to Alaska."

"Alaska?"

"Yep. He said he wanted to get as far away from there as he could, and he moved up to Alaska. We talked every now and then. I tried to check in on him to make sure he was all right. That was in 1971. Thirty-nine years ago."

"And you haven't seen him since?" Frank asked.

"A few weeks ago, he called me. He said he had found something important."

"What was it?"

"He said he found God."

Chapter 19

Alaska---Three Weeks Earlier

Sinclair Alderson staggered out the front door of the Big Dog Sports Bar and careened his way down the sidewalk. His feet didn't respond when he told them to move in a straight line, and he took as many steps sideways as he did forward. The buzz inside his head was just enough to convince him he was still alive.

He had lurched down this sidewalk many times in the past thirty-nine years, his feet remembering the way home even if his brain wasn't in gear. But the air seemed different tonight, dense and closing in on him to make him feel heavy, even though he was still a trim hundred and seventy pounds. He swatted at the mosquitos that were attracted to the smell of sweat and alcohol that hung over him like a veil.

He was wearing an unbuttoned blue work shirt over his T-shirt, and as he passed the wrought iron fence in front of a small house, his shirt caught on one of the spikes and jerked him to a halt. He muttered an obscenity at the fence and yanked his arm free. The shirt tore, and he stood still, looking stupidly at the rip in the sleeve until he couldn't remember why he was looking at it at all.

He muttered something about life being unfair and stumbled forward.

When he got to Ballister Street, he tried to negotiate the turn, but his feet tangled with each other and he fell headlong into the ditch beside the road. He made a little attempt to get up, thought better of it, and laid his head down.

The aroma of fresh-brewed coffee found its way into Sinclair's consciousness. He tried to remember where he was or what day it was, but the hammering inside his skull wouldn't let him concentrate.

His eyelids refused to move, but somehow he managed to squint one crusted eye open just enough to be shocked by the bright sunlight. He shut the eye, then tried again. Barely opening both eyes, he saw a beam of sunlight and everything around him was white. He wondered if he was dead and this was that white tunnel people talked about. But who would be serving coffee in the afterlife?

He had a vague memory of a ditch with a muddy bottom, and he tried to turn on his side to lift himself out of it like he had done so many times before. He moved his hand to push himself up, but his palm fell on something soft, and when he looked, he saw that he was lying on a clean, white sheet.

"Well, good morning." A deep, resonant voice invaded the room, and with it an even stronger odor of coffee. "Glad to see you're awake."

Sinclair blinked hard and tried to focus on the face that had positioned itself beside the bed. His words came out like a stream of gravel. "Where am I?"

The voice chuckled. "You're in my house, humble though it may be."

Sinclair rubbed his eyes and pushed himself up in the bed enough to see the big man sitting in a chair next to the bed. He looked like the picture Sinclair remembered of Paul Bunyan he once saw in a book. Red plaid shirt and dark beard around a weathered face. This had to be a dream. Or maybe he had died after all.

"I'd offer you a cup of coffee, but you're in no condition to drink it while you're lying in bed. When you feel like it, you can come in the kitchen. I've got some breakfast for you. It's not much, but I think you'll like it." He paused. "That is, if you can keep any food down. I've never seen anybody as wasted as you were last night."

Sinclair watched as the big man rose from the chair, his enormous torso looming in the bright morning light. "Who are you?" Sinclair asked.

"Most people call me Pastor John. When you feel like you can get up, bathroom's down there." He nodded his head toward the hall at the end of the bed. "Take your time. I've got nothing better to do today than to save a soul." Then he left.

Sinclair tried to sit up. On the third try, he managed to get his body upright enough to swing his legs over the side of the bed. He sat there for several minutes with his head in his hands, trying to make the room stop spinning. Finally, he looked around the small space that was fitted with a couple of chairs and the cot he was sitting on. He looked down at the clean sheets and marveled that anything could be so white. Certainly nothing he had slept on for years.

He picked up the feather pillow that had soothed his drunken head all night and held it to his chest like a close friend that he couldn't let go. When he thought he was sturdy enough, he put the pillow down, grasped the metal bar at the foot of the bed, unbent himself into something close to a standing position, and shuffled toward the bathroom.

His mouth felt like it was filled with cotton balls. He held onto the porcelain sink with one hand and splashed cold water on his face with the other until he could breathe again. Then he examined himself in the mirror. There was a cut on his forehead, just beneath the hairline, and a slit of caked blood stood out against his gray buzz cut. "Disgusting drunk," he said aloud to the mirror. His cheeks were sunken and his pale blue eyes had a hollowness to them that reminded him of his father and made him want to throw up.

He noticed he was wearing a clean T-shirt that was too big for him, but he was still dressed in his blue jeans. Memory of the Big Dog Sports Bar was a sickening swirl of smoke and laughter and beer and bourbon. Then nothing until he woke up in this stranger's home.

He tucked the T-shirt into his blue jeans and followed the smell of fresh coffee and frying bacon.

* * *

The big man in the red plaid shirt lifted slices of bacon from an oversized frying pan. "How do you like your coffee?" he asked.

"Black and bitter." Sinclair sank into one of the chairs at the small kitchen table where two place settings had been laid out. Like everything else he had seen in this house, the kitchen had a bright, cheerful look, with sunlight-yellow curtains above the sink billowing out with the breeze. He resisted the urge to put his head in his hands again.

Pastor John placed a mug of coffee in front of Sinclair and loaded up a large platter with scrambled eggs, biscuits, and bacon. He placed the dish in the middle of the table and took a seat opposite Sinclair. "Before we eat, I'd like to offer a word of thanks to our Creator for giving us this life and this food."

Before he could stop himself, Sinclair let out a cynical "huh," but his host didn't seem to notice.

The big man bowed his head and prayed exactly as he said he would, then looked up and pushed the platter in Sinclair's direction. "Help yourself."

Sinclair spooned half of the eggs and bacon onto his plate and picked up a biscuit, but before he bit into it, he looked up. "Thank you for your kindness," he said and wondered where the words came from. He couldn't remember thanking anybody for anything for such a long time. He took a bite. Maybe this was heaven after all.

Pastor John sat back in his chair, watching his guest shovel food into his mouth. "Hungry, eh?"

Sinclair swallowed a gulp of coffee and nodded. "Guess I hadn't eaten anything for a while. Maybe that's why I got so drunk last night." He shook his head.

"So you don't normally drink that much?"

Sinclair was getting ready to down a second biscuit, but his hand stopped halfway to his mouth. He put the biscuit on his plate.

Pastor John peered over the top of his coffee mug as he took a sip. "Most men I know who drink too much are trying to forget something." He put his cup down. "What's troubling you, Sinclair?"

Sinclair stared at the other man. "How'd you know my name?"

"It's on your driver's license. I looked at it last night to see if I should drive you home, but I decided you'd be better off here."

Sinclair wiped his hands on his blue jeans. The man across the table sat patiently, sipping coffee and waiting.

"Everybody has problems, Sinclair. Alcohol isn't the answer."

"It is for me." Sinclair raised his chin. "It's the only way I can forget."

"God can help you face the past." The man leaned forward and put his arms on the table. His eyes seemed to bore right through Sinclair.

Sinclair pushed his chair away from the table and stood.

"Thanks for the breakfast and for the sermon," he snorted out, "but there's nothing God can do for me. I'll be going."

The big man stood and looked down at his guest. "You can do whatever you want to, Sinclair, but I'm telling you right now that you can either go on drinking yourself to death, or you can face your past and allow God to heal you. It's your choice and you're the only one who can make it."

Sinclair didn't just hear the words. He felt them. They reached into his being and shattered the wall he had spent a lifetime building. His legs went watery, and he sank back down into the chair. "The only way God can heal me is if He'd bring somebody back from the dead."

* * *

Pastor John poured another cup of coffee for Sinclair. "Tell me about it."

Sinclair looked across the table at the big man with the soft brown eyes, and he began to talk about his little sister, Lacey.

Pastor John listened patiently, nodding as Sinclair explained his sister's learning disability and how that made her special.

"You wouldn't believe how sensitive she was to the animals that lived in the forest behind our home. She spent a lot of time back there. She liked to collect rocks and pine cones. Useless stuff. But they were like treasure to her, and she would come home with her pockets full of things and tell me stories about how the animals talked to her." He smiled sadly. "If I had been there instead of Vietnam, she wouldn't be dead."

"You don't know that, Sinclair. Besides, you can't help it if you were off fighting in Vietnam."

"That's just it. I didn't get drafted. I signed up to get away from my old man. He was the most useless piece of trash God ever made. He was always drinking and yelling at Mom. She used to take up *for him and told me to be patient and everything would work out, but I knew better.*

"*I shoulda stayed for Lacey's sake.*" *His eyes grew moist, and he pushed a tear off his cheek.* "*When I got back to the house after I was discharged, my parents were gone. They had moved away and didn't even tell me where they were going. The sheriff there told me Lacey had died in an accident, but I don't believe that.*" *He put his hands on the sides of his head and pushed as if he could destroy the awful thought inside.* "*If I had been there, she'd be alive.*"

Pastor John folded his hands together on top of the table. "*We'd all like to go back and have a chance to do things over, Sinclair.*" *He leaned forward.* "*What do you want God to do for you?*"

Sinclair stifled a sob. "*I want peace. And I want justice for Lacey.*"

The big man leaned back. "*Have you prayed and asked God?*"

Sinclair pressed his mouth into a thin line across his face. "*No, I never pray. I rage and rant and curse and drink myself into a stupor. But I never pray.*"

Pastor John lowered himself down to his knees on the hard kitchen floor. "*Pray with me now.*"

* * *

When Pastor John stopped his van in front of Sinclair's trailer, he turned to his new friend. "*Whatever you decide, I'd like you to keep me informed. I'll do anything I can to help.*" *He handed Sinclair a piece of paper with his phone number on it.*

Sinclair nodded. He stepped out of the car and strode to the trailer. Then he turned and saluted Pastor John.

Inside, he went immediately to the closet and pulled out the cardboard box that contained Lacey's belongings. Right on top was her little Bible with the zipper around it. He took it out, unzipped it, and opened it. He had to look at the Table of Contents to find the book of John that Pastor John had directed him to. As he flipped through the pages, a piece of paper fell out. He picked up the note and read the scrawled message.

Sinclair sat for a long time looking at the note and back at the Bible. His hands trembled. Then he called Charlie Deakin.

Chapter 20

The Box

"Where is Sinclair now?" I asked.

Uncle Charlie shook his head. "I don't know. A couple of weeks after the phone call, he showed up on my front porch and handed me a little metal box. He said it contained something valuable that had to do with Lacey's death, something that might prove she was murdered, and he wanted me to keep it hidden just in case he turned up anything.

"We walked out to the barn and hid it in the false bottom of Dan's tack box. I figured nobody would ever find it there. I suggested he call Ruddy Buchanan. He's the sheriff in Tabor County. They talked on the phone, and Sinclair said he was going down to Balmoral County to talk to the authorities there. That's where he lived with his parents. He stayed overnight and left the next day."

"How long ago was that?" I asked.

Uncle Charlie shook his head. "What day is it today?"

"Saturday, August 14."

"It was last Monday that he showed up at my door. I talked

him into staying overnight, and he left Tuesday afternoon. He said he wanted to drive down there to talk to the sheriff and poke around his old home."

"Has he contacted you since he left?"

"He called on Wednesday, but I must have been out in the barn, so he left a message. He said he'd talked to the sheriff over in Balmoral County Tuesday afternoon, and he was on his way to Willard County to talk to the sheriff there. I tried to call him back a few times, but it just rolled over to voice mail. That's not unusual for Sinclair, though. He's a loner."

Frank stopped writing long enough to look up. "That fits. Ruddy told me about the cold case telephone call. That's when he asked me to fly over and interview you."

"If you haven't been able to get in touch with him since he left that message, Sinclair doesn't know the box was stolen," I said.

"Not unless he found out some other way. But I doubt that. I expect he'll come back to the house, and I'll have to tell him those scumbags stole the box."

"So the bad guys have won the day." I shook my head.

"Not exactly," Uncle Charlie said.

Frank and I snapped to attention.

"What do you mean?" Frank asked.

"I got to thinking that it might be prudent to know what was in that box, so I opened it."

All the air went out of the room as Frank and I waited to hear what he'd discovered. "All it had was a piece of paper with some writing on it and a handkerchief that was embroidered with the letter R. I made a copy of the note and put the original and the handkerchief back in the box." He rubbed his eyes.

"Where is the copy of the note?" Frank asked.

Uncle Charlie pointed to the floor. "Honey," he said to me, "hand me my boots."

* * *

I hauled his size thirteen boots up and handed them to him. He pasted a Cheshire cat expression on his face, reached into the right boot, and pulled out an insole. Then he reached in again and came out with a piece of paper and handed it to me.

I read it and handed it to Frank. He glanced at it and his eyebrows headed north. He looked back at me. "What the heck does this have to do with a possible murder?"

Uncle Charlie shook his head. "Good question. When I made the copy of it, I thought maybe Sinclair had finally gone off his rocker."

I took the paper back and turned it over. "Sinclair thought this was a clue to his sister's death? That's ridiculous."

"Read it to me, Cassie," Uncle Charlie said.

"It says, 'The prince brought the princess in the wild wood.' There's a cross at the end of the sentence and a date at the top of the page." I took a picture of the note with my phone.

"What's the date?" Frank asked.

"August 12, 1970."

Uncle Charlie and Frank looked at me like they expected some brilliant insight to pour out of my head. "Got any ideas?" Frank said.

"Maybe Sinclair had some kind of mental breakdown or something. Could be the effects of PTSD. It happens."

"I know." Uncle Charlie frowned. "But if it's just a child's scribbled note, why did somebody want to kill me for it?"

Frank and I looked at each other. "We need to find Sinclair," he said. He took his phone out of his pocket and walked to the side of Uncle Charlie's bed. "But before we do anything else, I have a couple of pictures I'd like you to look at. Do you think you're up to it?"

"Son, I'm alive and awake. I feel like I can do just about

anything." He gestured toward the night table. "Cassie, see if you can find my glasses."

I got his bifocals from the bedside stand and handed them to him.

Frank scrolled on his phone and held it in front of Uncle Charlie's face.

Uncle Charlie adjusted his glasses and took Frank's phone in his hand. I leaned over to see what was on the screen. It was a picture of the man we had found by the barn.

Uncle Charlie stared at it a long time, then he looked up. "He looks dead," he said.

"He is."

"That's Shorty. Who killed him?"

"We don't know that. Did you get off any shots?"

"I wish I had, but I didn't have a firearm out there in the barn."

Frank jotted something in his notebook. "We think his buddy shot him. Maybe because the horse had disabled him and he realized he was stuck with an invalid who couldn't make it back to the bike."

"Shows you how low those two were," Uncle Charlie spat out. "They didn't even take care of their own." He handed the phone back to Frank.

Frank tapped on the screen a couple of times and held it up in front of Uncle Charlie again. "Here's another one. Recognize him?"

Uncle Charlie stared at the image on the phone. "I'm not sure. He could be the second guy in the barn. The big one. But when I saw him, he was wearing a kerchief on his head and he had a couple of day's growth of beard. This fella looks clean-shaven."

I asked to look at the picture and recognized the policeman they had shot at the hospital.

"If you had a picture of his hands, I'd be more sure," Uncle Charlie said.

Frank scrolled some more on his phone and handed it back.

"Yeah. This is the other one. See that? It's part of a tattoo he had on his arm. Some kind of scorpion. I noticed it when they came into the barn the first time. Do you know where this guy is?"

"He's in the morgue," Frank said without any emotion.

Uncle Charlie's eyelids drooped, and I saw his jaw tighten. "I've killed men," he said in a low tone. "I'm not proud of it, but when we were in Nam, I thought I was doing it to protect something precious." He sighed. "The Vietcong were trying to kill me for the same reason. I can't find it in my heart to blame them."

He turned his gaze back to the phone. "But those punks who robbed me were willing to kill for their own underhanded purposes. I can't tell you how much I despise that." He squinted his eyes until they were almost shut. "I hate to say it about a fellow human being, but I'm glad those two aren't on this earth anymore."

Frank let the silence hang in the room for a few seconds before he continued. "Any idea how they knew about the box? Do you think your friend Sinclair could have told them?"

"Could be. When Sinclair left my place, he said he was going to talk to the authorities and then go back to the place he grew up."

"Do you think somebody could have forced the information from Sinclair? You know, tortured him or something?"

"I guess so, but it's just hard for me to believe Sinclair would have given anybody an idea about this. Maybe he got drunk or high and spilled the beans. I just don't know."

We were all silent for a minute. Then Uncle leaned his head against the pillow and sighed. "Cassie, I want you to do something for me."

"Anything."

"Get me out of this place. I want to go home."

Nurse Ratched walked in just as he uttered that last remark. "We'll let you go as soon as you're able." She held up a little cup.. "But for now, I have a few pills for you."

Uncle Charlie made a face, but I could see he was exhausted.

The nurse turned to me. "Your friend Ralph is out in the hall with two of the biggest people I have ever seen."

Uncle Charlie winked at me. "Go tell those bikers I said hello." He yawned. "I'm going to get a little shut-eye."

Chapter 21

The Brotherhood

Frank and I went into the hall and found Ralph with Buck and Archie, two of the bikers who had helped us when Frank was in danger.

Frank shook hands with the big guys, and each of them gave me a hug that pressed the air out of my lungs and left me gasping. I made a mental note to never make them mad.

Most of Ralph's friends are big and strong, but these two, Buck and Archie, are on the massively muscular end of the scale. They looked like they could pick the hospital up and move it to another town if they wanted to. But in reality, they were quiet and gentle.

Buck had saddlebags full of books. After he learned I was an English major in college, he and I spent hours talking about nineteenth-century British literature. His favorite author was Anthony Trollope.

Archie could knit. He told me it took his mind off his problems and lowered his blood pressure. He showed me a sweater he was making for his sister's little girl. It was pink with little crocheted flowers sewn to the pockets. I asked him if he'd teach me to knit.

In the little time I had known them, I learned that they were committed to a life of independence. No drugs and no alcohol. Although they never confided in me, I gathered their group of bikers had had problem lives, but chose to deal with it in this way. They called themselves the Brotherhood.

Frank left to call Ruddy Buchanan, and Ralph went outside to check something on his bike. Buck, Archie, and I wandered around to the hospital cafeteria, got some food, and found a little table in the corner.

They wanted to know how my uncle was doing. Ralph had told them about the assault on Uncle Charlie and that bikers were apparently responsible.

I sipped coffee while they wolfed down egg salad sandwiches. "I can't believe bikers would have done that," I said.

Archie wiped his mouth. "There're bad dudes in every group," he said. "You can't trust anybody these days."

"Yeah. That's what people keep telling me."

I told them about how a friend of Uncle Charlie's had asked him to hide something at the farm, but I didn't let on about what it was. The more I thought about it, the crazier it seemed to me. Sinclair must have lost a few cards in his deck. Some people do that after they've suffered for a long time.

"If it was just between your uncle and his friend," Buck asked, "how did the thieves know where it was?"

"His friend must have told somebody else," I said. "That's the only thing that makes any sense."

"Probably a woman," Archie said.

Buck snickered. "He should've talked to you, bro. You could have given him a dissertation on being used by women."

Archie actually blushed. He shrugged and looked at me. "I've been on the receiving end of the feminine gambit," he said. "Buck is kind enough to remind me of it now and then."

Buck made a fist and hit Archie on the shoulder. "Just givin' you a hard time," he said. "It never hurts to remember our mistakes."

"I don't understand," I said. "You guys are smart. How could you fall for something so obvious as a woman trying to use you?"

"Men like to show off, Cassie," Archie said. "Especially in front of a woman. You wouldn't believe how many stupid things I've done in my life to try to impress some girl."

"And it's not just about women," Buck said. "Men are competitive too. We want to prove we're better than the next guy." He turned toward Archie. "Remember that guy Clint who stopped at Ralph's place and was bragging about how well he could do the donut?"

"Oh yeah." Archie laughed and slapped his thigh.

"Wait," I said. "What donut?"

Archie leaned back. "A donut is when the rider makes the motorcycle spin in a circle. It's a tough stunt to do and some of the guys were talking about wanting to learn it when we were at Ralph's place."

Buck nodded. "Clint was this new guy who had just come in for the first time, and he started telling us how he was an expert at doing motorcycle stunts." His eyes sparkled. "He had had a few too many beers, and the guys were egging him on." He made a face. "It didn't end well."

"What happened?" I asked.

"Let's just say Clint left part of his hide on the road next to Ralph's place. The medics thought skin grafts would come in handy."

"Ouch."

Archie shrugged. "What can I say, Cassie? It's just plain old masculine stupidity. When we get together, we're always trying to one-up each other. You know, show the other guys how smart and clever you are. Before you know it, you've done something really dumb." He wagged his head back and forth. "Add a little alcohol into the mix, and a perfectly decent man will turn into a raving idiot."

"What happened to Clint?"

"Don't know," Buck replied. "We never saw him again."

Chapter 22

Plan for the Future

After Buck and Archie left, I decided to get some fresh air. Being outside gave me a jolt of optimism. Breathing in the dry air and having a chance to stretch my legs energized me.

I ran into Greg who was getting ready to return to the farm to see if there was anything they missed. He asked me if I'd like to go with him, and he motioned me over to an old pickup truck, opened the passenger door, and bowed low. "Your chariot awaits, m'lady," he said.

Greg's truck looked like it had lived a hard life. One of the fenders had a big dent, and the paint flaked around islands of rust. When he started it up, it bucked a few times before Greg got it to move forward. He turned down the radio that was blaring out country music. "Sorry about the ride," he said. "My Ferrari's in the shop."

We bounced along the road while I told him about our conversation with Uncle Charlie.

He looked pleased. "Frank said you got a lot of information

from him about the assault, and that he ID'd the two guys who tried to rob him."

"Right," I said.

Greg drove with one hand looped over the steering wheel and the other arm out the window, tapping the side of the truck in time with the music. "We got some good information from the lab."

"What did they find?"

"They matched the DNA samples from the grass to the guy who was impersonating a police officer. We're waiting on the lab to finalize identities."

When we got to the farm, we walked around the place looking for anything they might have missed. The horses were restless, so I suggested we turn them out into the paddock so they could get some exercise while I mucked out the stalls.

"What does it mean to muck out the stalls?" Greg said.

I laughed at the city boy. "You probably don't want to know." After we had taken the last horse out, I rolled a wheelbarrow up to Dan's stall and handed a pitchfork to Greg. "It's time for your first lesson in horsemanship."

We spent an hour cleaning stalls and laying down fresh straw. Then I filled water buckets while Greg tossed hay into each stall. We finished and sat down on one of the hay bales. Greg wiped the sweat off his forehead with the back of his hand.

"I never knew cleaning out horse manure could be so much fun," he said and leaned back against the side of the barn. I handed him a bottle of water I had retrieved from the refrigerator and watched him as he downed it in a few gulps. I liked this guy. He was unassuming and guileless. Like you could believe anything he told you.

While we rested from our efforts, Frank came strolling in. "They told me I'd find the two of you here."

"Hey man, where've you been?" Greg said. "You missed all the fun."

"So I see." Frank looked around at the newly cleaned stalls. "You getting a lesson in taking care of horses?" he asked Greg.

"These horses better appreciate me," Greg said. "I don't spend as much time cleaning my apartment as I did cleaning up their mess."

"I'm sure they love you for it." He turned to me. "How're you holding up?"

I shrugged. "I'm okay. It's nice to have some work to do."

"We need to talk about the arrangements once Charlie is released from the hospital," he said. "I've talked to Ruddy about putting a protective detail around him."

"Why?" I said. "The two guys who robbed him are both dead. The stuff they stole is long gone, and there's nothing of value around here anybody could want. I think Uncle Charlie and I will be just fine here on the farm."

"I disagree." Frank crossed his arms over his chest. *Surprise, surprise.* "Ruddy and I think either Greg or I should be present at all times. He's willing to give Greg a week to stay at the farm. I'll come by after work and spend the nights here." He looked over at Greg. "Is that okay with you, pard?"

"Sounds good to me." Greg's phone dinged. "Hold on. I need to take this." He put the phone to his ear and walked out of the barn to take the call.

Frank leaned against Dan's stall. "Cassie, I want to talk to you."

I hate it when somebody says they want to talk to me. It always —and I mean always—is something I don't want to talk about. I put a bored look on my face and brushed at the dust on my jeans. "About what?"

He picked up a straw from the bale and chewed on it. "Look, Cassie, we're going to have to work together ..."

Before he could finish, Greg bounded back inside the barn. "We got the lab results!"

That did the trick. Frank White likes nothing more than getting fingerprints and DNA results. He was on the phone to the lab before I could ignore him again.

"Let's head back to the hospital," I said to Greg. "I want to check on Uncle Charlie." And I didn't want to have a heart-to-heart with a man who didn't have a heart.

"Your wish is my command," Greg said and bowed. I was beginning to like being treated like a princess.

Chapter 23

Dolly and Fiddlesticks

A s Greg and I bumped along in his old truck on the way back to the hospital, I figured it was time to get the actual truth about Frank White. "Greg," I said. "What was it you were going to tell me about Frank yesterday at the diner when he interrupted us?"

"Oh, yeah." He pushed his hat back on his head. "There's something you should know about him. You see ..."

My phone dinged, and I held up a finger to shush him. "It's Dolly. I better take this."

I put her on speaker and introduced her to Greg.

"How's your uncle doing?" she asked.

"He's awake and may be discharged soon, so I'm going to stay out here at the farm to take care of Uncle Charlie until he can get back on his feet."

"Who's going to cook for the two of you?" she asked.

"Good question. That's not exactly my forte, and Uncle Charlie is going to need good nutritious meals. I can order food from one of the local restaurants."

"I'll come," she said.

"You can't come. You have a job."

"I have plenty of vacation time saved up—you know I never take a day off." I could hear her opening and closing cabinets, and I knew she was cleaning up the kitchen while she had me on speaker. "And the boss's niece has been pestering him to let her learn the business, so it's not a problem. Besides, Cassie, I owe you for letting me room here with practically no rent. I can do all the cooking and cleaning while you and your uncle try to figure out what's going on."

"It could be dangerous," I said.

"I've been thinking about that ever since you and I had that talk. My whole life has been locked in a florist shop in Newton. It wouldn't be right for me to stay all safe in my little cocoon while you and your uncle are in danger. Now's my chance to do a good deed, and I'm going to take it." I could imagine the huge, dimpled grin on her face.

I wasn't so sure this was a great idea. Dolly isn't exactly Xena the warrior princess. On the other hand, we sure would need somebody to help with the cooking and cleaning, so I agreed. "Do you want me to fly back over and pick you up?"

"No way. You know I'm never going to get in one of those little Barbie airplanes you fly. You give me directions and I'll drive over. What is it? A four- or five-hour drive?"

"That's about right." I asked her to bring some more clothes for me.

"Can I bring Fiddlesticks?" she asked.

"Sure. She'll love it. Lots of mice." I clicked off and looked over at Greg, who had been listening.

"Who's Fiddlesticks?" he asked.

"That's Dolly's cat." I rolled my eyes. "The most persnickety animal God ever made. She's an inside cat, made for the city. She'll probably go into trauma at the farm and hide all day in Dolly's room."

"Your roommate sounds nice," Greg said as we bounced along the county road. "Is she pretty?"

"You have no idea."

* * *

I spent the night at the hospital again. Frank and Greg didn't want me to be alone at the farm, and it seemed like a good idea to stay close to Uncle Charlie. I had dinner in the room with him while he told me stories about farm life.

The next morning, I returned to the farm to take care of the horses and wait for Dolly. When she rolled up in her old Honda CR-V, I met her on the porch. She got out carrying a little cage with her precious Fiddlesticks in it.

She put the cage down and gave me a hug. "I'm so glad you're safe. You had me worried." She made a sweeping gesture with her arm. "This is wonderful! I can see why you love it so much."

"Are you sure you want to do this?" I asked. "It's not exactly city life, and you won't see a lot of people while you're here. Just Uncle Charlie and a couple of the guys who are guarding him."

"I'm going to love it," she said. "Now let's get these groceries out of the car." We left Fiddlesticks in her cage while we unloaded Dolly's suitcases and the groceries she brought.

We took a quick tour through the house, and I explained there were only three bedrooms, so she and I would share one of them. Uncle Charlie had his room, and Frank and Greg would share the other one.

"No problem," she said as she eyed the furniture in the room we would share. I had the feeling she was already planning to make some decorative changes. She hung a few things in the closet and found an empty drawer in the dresser for her underclothes.

"So, there will be five of us?" I could see her calculating her grocery situation.

"Yes. Is that a problem?"

"Nope. I love cooking for a crowd." She waltzed into her favorite room, the kitchen. "And look at this kitchen!" Dolly was in her element. She opened cabinets and examined their contents. "A Sub-Zero refrigerator. This is my kind of place. I have a complete plan of nutritious meals."

Just then, we heard a plaintive meow coming from the front porch.

"Oops. I forgot all about Fiddles," Dolly said, and we went back to check on the feline prima donna.

Fiddlesticks was standing in her cage and looking very unhappy with the whole situation. Dolly went right into motherhood mode. "Oh, my poor little baby," she said as she opened the door to the cage and lifted Precious One out.

"You're going to love it here, sweetheart," she cooed as she held Miss Priss close to her heart. "Let's go inside."

Fiddlesticks took a look around and suddenly leaped out of Dolly's arms, ran to the end of the porch, and jumped down. She looked like she was on a mission. Dolly and I looked at each other in shock, and then we ran down the steps and around the side of the house.

"Fiddle! Fiddlesticks, come back," Dolly called as she negotiated the uneven ground in her faux Jimmy Choo sandals.

I caught sight of Fiddlesticks as she made a sharp turn into the barn. The inside cat had just made a career change.

By the time Dolly and I got to the barn, Fiddlesticks was marching down the aisle like she was deciding which horse she would grace with her company. She chose Dan.

I found the whole scene intensely amusing, but Dolly looked alarmed to see her little kitty-poo take to farm life so quickly. Fiddlesticks jumped up on the wooden half door and gracefully floated down into Dan's stall.

"Oh, no. She'll be trampled," Dolly cried, and we ran over to look into the stall.

There was prissy little Fiddlesticks rubbing her back against big old Dan's forelegs while he put his head down to sniff and nuzzle her.

I smiled at Dolly. "Love at first sight. I guess it was just meant to be."

"I never would have believed it," Dolly said. "Do you think she'll be safe out here?"

"I suspect she'll have all the horses bowing down to her by sunset," I said. "And the mice will just have to find another farm."

That afternoon—two days after his surgery—we took Uncle Charlie home to his farm. The doctors were not happy that he was checking himself out.

"Don't worry, doc," Uncle Charlie said as I wheeled him to the exit. "I won't sue if anything goes wrong." He pointed toward the door. "Cassie, I see sunshine on the other side of that sliding glass door. Get me out of here and into that sun." I was afraid he might get up and boogie out to the parking lot.

Frank and Greg helped me get him into the Tabor County Sheriff office's Ford Explorer. Frank let me drive with Uncle Charlie in the passenger seat. When we pulled the car up to the farmhouse, I turned to Uncle Charlie and said in my most cheerful voice, "We're home!"

His eyes went moist.

"Hold on, old timer," Frank said. "I want to get something before you go in the house." He hopped out of the back seat and disappeared while Greg and I helped Uncle out of the car. By the time we got him situated and ready to walk, Frank appeared around the side of the house, walking Old Dan toward the car.

Uncle Charlie dropped my hand and limped toward the big gelding. Dan whinnied and dragged Frank forward. He lowered his head so Uncle could scratch behind his ears and rub his face. I heard Uncle whisper, "You saved me, old boy. I owe you."

The front door opened and Dolly popped out in a sky blue dress with a white apron tied around her waist. "Welcome home, Uncle Charlie," she called out.

Uncle Charlie had never met Dolly. I had told him she'd be staying with us to help out, but I don't think he expected to see the mirage that was standing on his front porch with her arms spread wide. He handed Dan's lead line to me and limped toward the house.

Greg looked thunderstruck. He blinked hard. "I think I'm gonna enjoy this assignment."

Chapter 24

Ronnie Bradwell

The aroma of tomato sauce was powerful as we stepped into the house. Dolly fussed around Uncle Charlie, making him sit in his recliner and telling him about the healthy foods she was making for him.

"Why, Dolly, you don't have to go to all this trouble for me," he said. "You have your own life to live."

"It's no trouble at all. I've always wanted to see what it was like to live on a farm."

"Great," Uncle said. "Your curiosity is my good fortune."

"I saw some casseroles in the freezer. Looks like you've been busy cooking for yourself," she said.

"I'm not much of a cook. Doesn't run in the Deakin family." He winked at me. "There's a nice lady who lives in town and she brings food over now and then, in return for me doing some work around her house."

Frank raised his eyebrows. "Who is she?" he asked.

"Her name's Veronica Bradwell."

"You never told me about her," I said and tried to keep my voice under control.

Uncle Charlie looked down and fumbled with his hands. "I just met her recently," he said. He cleared his throat and turned his attention back to Dolly. "But I'm looking forward to your cooking, Dolly. Cassie tells me you're practically a French chef."

Dolly waved a dismissive hand. "That Cassie. She's always exaggerating. We just want to give you good food so you can heal fast." She headed for the kitchen. "I better check the tomato sauce. We're having spaghetti and meatballs tonight."

"Can I get you anything, Uncle?"

"You already got me the best thing I can have, Cassie. You brought me home. Now you go help that young lady in the kitchen. Maybe you'll be the first Deakin who learned how to cook."

Just as I stood, the doorbell rang. We had all agreed to be extra cautious if anyone came to the farm. Frank slipped his jacket on over the shoulder holster, and I answered the door with him beside me.

The woman standing on the porch looked like she was around forty years old but trying to pass for thirty. Her long auburn hair was stylishly cut, and she was wearing a pink and white sundress that was tied around her waist, outlining a shapely torso. She was holding a covered dish.

Right away, I noticed her hands. You don't see a lot of women in the farmlands who have well-manicured hands with long fingernails polished pink.

She looked surprised when we opened the door, but she recovered nicely. "I'm Veronica Bradwell," she said. "I'm a friend of Charles Deakin's. Is he in?"

Uncle Charlie's voice boomed from behind us. "Come on in, Ronnie."

As the vision in pink stepped across the threshold, she deftly removed her sunglasses and I noticed clear blue eyes and very curly eyelashes.

She glided past Frank and me and over to Uncle Charlie. "My poor Charles," she exclaimed. "I just heard about your accident this morning. I called the hospital right away, and they said you'd been sent home."

Accident? I wondered who told her that.

She managed to balance the dish on one hand while she leaned over to give Uncle Charlie a peck on the cheek. Quite an accomplishment. Uncle Charlie's face turned the same color pink as her dress.

She straightened up and glanced back at us. "I didn't realize you had so much company, Charles," she said.

Uncle Charlie looked our way to offer the introductions. "This is Mrs. Bradwell." When Dolly came in from the kitchen, Veronica's eyes scanned her up and down, and her smile thinned out. He introduced me last of all. "Ronnie, this is my niece, Cassie. I've told you about her."

"Cassie? Of course. I hope we can become good friends."

That seemed like an assumption on her part that we'd be seeing more of each other.

She held the dish out to me. "It's a peach pie. I think there's enough for everyone."

"Ronnie makes the best peach pie in the universe," Uncle Charlie announced. "Let's have some now with coffee."

"Dessert before dinner?" I asked.

"Yes," Uncle Charlie said. "We're celebrating."

Mrs. Bradwell pulled the rocking chair up next to Uncle Charlie and leaned in. She placed her hand gently on his arm in a gesture that looked to me like it was familiar to both of them. "What in the world happened, Charles?" Her voice was low and soft. I could barely make out the words. "I want to know everything."

Dolly and I retreated to the kitchen, and Frank followed. I guess the sugar-coated Mrs. Bradwell was a bit too sweet, even for him. We left Greg in the living room to monitor the situation.

Dolly took the aluminum foil off the pie. "This certainly looks good," she said and pinched off a tiny piece of crust. "Yum. Very tasty. Mrs. Bradwell is definitely a wonderful cook."

"What's that figure carved into the crust?" Frank asked. "Looks like a four-pointed star."

"Yes, I see what you mean," Dolly said. "Some women like to have a kind of signature to their most special dish. Maybe this is hers."

Frank leaned against the kitchen counter and crossed his arms over his chest. "What's your special dish, Cassie?"

"Toast," I shot back. "I'm excellent at making toast."

He grinned at me. "I like toast."

I ignored the comment and handed him a spatula. "Use your best detective skills to cut the pie into six slices, please."

While Frank was working on a geometrically perfect slicing of the pie and Dolly was spooning grounds into the coffee maker, I busied myself getting plates and silverware while I tried to decipher the sounds coming from the next room. I couldn't quite make out the verbal pas de deux, but I heard Ronnie's lilting whispers followed by Uncle Charlie's lower, firmer voice. By the time we returned, their heads were bent together, almost touching, and Ronnie was punctuating every one of Uncle Charlie's sentences with gasps of "Oh no" and "Horrors!"

Oh, brother.

We had our dessert and coffee, and I had to admit it was the best peach pie I had ever tasted. So Veronica Bradwell was a good cook. I tried not to imagine what else she was good at.

"I better get the horses back into the barn," I said and stood up. "It might rain." I hoped no one noticed there wasn't a cloud in the sky.

Chapter 25

I'm Not Angry

Frank followed me out of the house and caught up with me as I crossed the yard to the paddock. "That was quite a show," he said. "What do you make of her?"

"She looks like the kind of person who'd wear a frilly pink nightgown," I said and tossed my head. "You probably know the type. A tart."

Frank stopped by the gate. "A tart. Now there's a word you don't hear every day."

"If the nightgown fits ..." I opened the gate and waited as Dan and Blondie trotted to us. I've never understood why horses seem so eager to return to the barn. You'd think they'd want to stay out in the field where they could run and play, but every time I open the gate to collect them, they come running home.

We walked the horses into the barn and settled them into their stalls. "Hand me Dan's brush, would you? Looks like he rolled in the dirt. I want to get some of it off him."

Frank handed me the brush and stood at the door of the stall, watching me. "Cassie," he said, "why are you so angry?"

"I'm not angry," I said as I took a fierce swipe at the dirt on

Dan's withers. "Uncle Charlie can do whatever he wants with whoever he wants to. It's a free country." For some reason, I could not have a polite conversation with this man. He brought out the worst in me. Every time I opened my mouth, the words came out sarcastic or just plain mean.

"I'm not talking about her." Frank motioned toward the house. "Why are you so angry with me?"

I stopped brushing and stared at him in exasperation. "You know exactly why I'm angry."

"No, I don't."

"Yes, you do."

"I don't."

"You do." My voice was climbing into the outer edges of the atmosphere again.

"Cassie, stop it. You're sounding like a …"

"What? Like a woman?"

He opened the stall door and stepped in. "Sorry. I didn't mean that. It's just that I want us to be friends, but I don't understand what's going on."

I leaned against Dan's massive bulk and crossed my arms over my chest. "You stood me up." I could feel my face turning red, but I didn't care. "I sat in that restaurant waiting for you for over an hour. I had to put up with the waiter's pitying look every time he came to the table and asked if I wanted another glass of wine."

Frank took a step backward as if he was genuinely surprised. "I did not stand you up."

"Ha!" I snorted so loud, Dan twitched and turned his big head around to look at me. "I believe that's what you call it when you don't show up for a date." I threw my arm out to the side and banged my hand into one of the wooden planks in Dan's stall. "Ouch." I shook my hand. "Darn it. See what you made me do."

He walked over and held my sore hand. "I was called in to an emergency, and we weren't allowed to use our phones. I texted you as soon as I could and explained what happened."

"You expect me to believe that?" I huffed out. "That's the lamest excuse I've ever heard."

"I wanted to have dinner with you, Cassie. Why would I lie?"

I jerked my hand away. "I think it's the masculine thing to do when you get a better deal somewhere else."

His jaw dropped. "No self-respecting man would do that."

"Oh no? Well, I've known a couple of men who did just that." It happened to me when I was sixteen years old and the cutest boy in the class invited me to the prom. My friend told me he had broken up with his beauty queen girlfriend, and so I got the nod, even though I was nerdy, studious Cassie, and probably the only girl in the school without a date. The afternoon of the prom, he called and told me his dad had grounded him so he couldn't go.

When I got to school the next week, I found out he'd lied. He had made up with his girlfriend and took her to the prom. Everybody in school knew about it. That was my first real lesson in humiliation, and I learned it well. "Most men I know are egotistical and arrogant." I rubbed my hand against my blue jeans. "And untrustworthy."

Frank stared at me intensely. "I'm not like that, Cassie," he said quietly. "You know me better than that." He reached for my hand again, but I pulled away.

"I don't know you at all," I declared, and shoved the brush at him. "Would you mind cleaning the dirt off Dan? I need some time alone." I walked out of the barn.

I wandered into the fields. This was a sabbatical year when Uncle Charlie let the land rest. The dried remnants of last year's crop lay all around me like reminders of broken promises. Something brushed against my foot and made me jump. I looked down to see Fiddlesticks walking beside me. "Fiddlesticks? What are you doing? I thought you didn't like me."

The cat purred and rubbed herself against my leg. I sat down cross-legged on the ground, and she climbed into my lap and let me stroke her back. Maybe I smelled like Dan.

"You seem to know the secret for changing your life when you find yourself in a new place, Fiddlesticks," I said to her. "I wish you'd tell me how to do that."

Chapter 26

Ruddy Assigns Frank

Things were still tense between Frank and me when we got into the Ford Explorer on Monday morning.

"Do you know why Sheriff Buchanan wants to see me?" I asked Frank. After my scorned woman act from the day before, I was trying to be on good behavior.

Frank's face was without expression. Another thing I hate about him. I can't make him mad. "He wants to see you because Charles Deakin is your uncle and I'm assigned to investigate the crime. Since you and I happened onto the scene together, Ruddy wants to talk to you." We drove in silence to the Tabor County sheriff's office in Bridgeton.

Frank turned the car into a dirt parking lot and stopped under the shade of an enormous oak tree. "That's the sheriff's office," he said and pointed to a modern building on the right.

I got out of the car and managed to trip over one of the roots of the tree.

Frank came around and took my arm. I guess he was just trying to keep me upright, at least until we got inside. I made a mental note to watch where I put my feet for the rest of my life.

"Pretty nice place for a sheriff's office," I said.

"Ruddy's father was a medical doctor," he said. "He left this office to the county when he died and specified that it be used for a sheriff's office."

"Great. Maybe I can have my blood pressure checked while we're here."

He gave a semi-laugh and released my arm when we got to the door. Inside was a large, bright room. The lady sitting behind the desk was middle-aged. Her hair was streaked with gray, cropped short, and pushed behind her ears. She was wearing a long-sleeve plaid shirt and leaning over a book that was open on her desk. She looked up when she heard us come in, and I had the feeling I'd seen her somewhere before.

"Hey, Shirley," Frank said. "Whatcha reading?"

"Well, hey there, young man," she drawled. She held up a well-worn copy of *The Iliad*.

I liked her right away. I liked the way she talked, and that she was reading one of my favorite stories. "It looks like you've read that copy a few times," I said.

"I read it at least once a year," she said. "Makes me feel good to know those people back in the day were a lot more violent than we are."

She stood and I was surprised at how tall she was. Close to six feet, I guessed. Her plaid shirt was tucked into a pair of blue jeans. She stuck out a hand. "I'm Shirley."

"Cassie Deakin." I took her hand and felt the rough calluses. You don't get those from sitting in an office, and I immediately thought of Annie Oakley and wondered if Shirley had a second life as a sharp-shooting rodeo performer.

"Good to meet ya, Cassie. Ruddy told me about the shooting. How's your uncle?"

"He'll be fine."

"Ruddy's expecting the two of you." She lifted the handset on her phone and punched a button. "Frank and Cassie are here," she shouted into the receiver as if she didn't believe in the transmission of sound through wires. She nodded when she got a response. "He'll be right out."

A minute later, Ruddy Buchanan appeared at the entrance to a hall. Without his cowboy hat on, I saw a full head of dark hair, cut short. He was wearing a solid blue shirt, dark blue jeans, and cowboy boots. His sheriff's badge glinted off his shirt pocket.

He stood at the doorway for a moment just looking at the two of us with those intense hazel eyes, then gestured for us to follow him. "Come on back to the office," he said. "Shirley, I don't want to be disturbed."

"Yes sir, Master of the Universe," she said and saluted him. Then she gave an eye roll aimed at me, a little woman-to-woman gesture that I liked. I turned my head back to smile at her so the men couldn't see as I followed them down the hall.

"Shirley is my sister," Ruddy said over his shoulder as we walked down the hall. He opened the door to his office and motioned us inside. "Older sister. She still thinks she's in charge."

That's what I recognized in her. She had the same color hazel eyes. "She seems nice," I said sweetly.

He arched an eyebrow and looked down at me as I passed by him. "She's the most hard-headed, stubborn woman God ever put on this earth," he said. "But she is nice. I'll give you that."

He walked behind his desk and pointed to two chairs in front and we sat. "May I call you Cassie?" he asked.

"Yes, of course."

"How's your uncle doing?"

"He's happy to be back home."

Ruddy Buchanan was an imposing figure, whether in the field or standing behind his desk. He was a little taller than his sister and obviously spent some time at the gym. Probably both of them did.

He took a seat, and I tried to guess his age. I decided on mid-forties. But the most impressive thing about him was the forcefulness of his gaze. He had a way of looking at you without blinking until you began to feel uncomfortable. He aimed that visual scrutiny at me, and I wanted to look away, but I figured this was some kind of test, so I stared back. I tried not to blink, but my eyes got so dry they hurt, so I finally gave in.

He broke off then and turned to Frank. "Let's talk about the assault on Charles Deakin."

Frank nodded. "Yes, sir." He took out his small notebook and pen.

"Frank, like I told you, I want you to head up the investigation into this crime. I want to know why those men targeted Mr. Deakin. If they were working on their own, the case is over since they're both dead. But I have a feeling that they were there on somebody else's orders or others were involved. If that's the case, I want to know who ordered them and why."

Frank jotted notes. He filled Ruddy in on the information Uncle Charlie had given us about Sinclair.

Buchanan sat back in his chair. "Do you have a copy of the paper they stole?"

"I took a photo of it," I said and handed him my phone.

He stared at the image for a long time. "Cassie, does this make any sense to you?" he asked.

He surprised me by asking my opinion, and I liked it. "No. Not at all. I think Sinclair was just grasping at straws because he felt bad about his sister's death."

"That may be true," he said and looked back down at the image on my phone again, "but I've seen things stranger than this that solved a murder. I don't think you can disregard Sinclair's gut feeling." He handed the phone back to me and turned his attention to Frank.

"What about the handkerchief that was in the box?"

"It's gone. Charlie told us it was a plain white handkerchief with the letter R embroidered on it in red, but he didn't copy it."

"That's too bad," Ruddy said. "Where is Sinclair now?"

"We don't know," Frank said. "He called Charlie last Wednesday and left a message that he had talked to the sheriff in Balmoral County. He said he was going to snoop around some more and then go talk to the sheriff in Willard County, but he never called back. Charlie's been trying to contact him, but his phone must be turned off. Charlie says that's not unusual, but now he's concerned for Sinclair's safety because of the robbery and assault."

Ruddy sat quietly for a minute. He was one of those people who wasn't afraid of silence. I liked that about him. When he was ready, he raised his head and looked at Frank. "Sinclair is obviously the key to this crime. If you can't get in touch with him, I'd like you to go over to Balmoral County and talk to Sheriff Easterly. He's a friend of mine, and he'll give you the straight story. Then go on to Willard County and talk to Bob Jessop. I don't know him as well as Easterly, but if he was the last person Sinclair talked to before he went quiet, you need to find out what was said." He tapped his fingers on the desk. "Follow Sinclair's steps and find him."

"Will do," Frank said and put the notebook away. "I'll call both of them this afternoon to set up appointments."

Ruddy turned his attention back to me. "Cassie, I'd like to deputize you."

"Me?" My head jerked up, and I felt my eyes go wide.

"Yes. You may not know Sinclair, but you have the knowledge of your uncle, and you can act as his eyes and ears. My sources tell me you're smart and dedicated."

I wondered just who these sources were. "Sheriff Buchanan, I appreciate your faith in me, but I decided a long time ago I wasn't cut out for law enforcement."

"I know all about that," he said and waved his hand like he was dismissing the notion. "I know you went through police training in an academy in Texas after you graduated from college. Your test scores and personal assessments were excellent, but you chose not to follow a career in law enforcement."

"How do you know that?" I was surprised he would take the time to check out my past.

"Law enforcement organizations share information with each other." He tapped a finger on the manila folder lying on his desk. "You told your instructors that you didn't believe you could ever use a gun on another human being and you felt that would disqualify you."

I felt my face grow hot, and I could feel Frank staring at me. Apparently, Ruddy hadn't shared this information with him.

"You don't have to carry a gun or get involved in a shoot-out. I just want your brain to be involved." He winked at me. "Frank can use all the brain power we can give him."

Ruddy Buchanan should have been a psychiatrist. He sat behind his desk with his elbows on the arms of his chair, hands folded together like he was waiting for me to realize I had no other choice but to do what he wanted me to. And he was right. Somehow he knew I wouldn't turn down a chance to solve the mystery behind the crime committed against my uncle. "All right," I said. "I'll help out."

He took a badge out of his desk drawer. "Please stand so I can swear you in."

With my new badge hooked onto my belt and an admonition that I was to take orders from Frank, I left Ruddy's office. Frank stayed behind to catch up on some other issues, so I returned to the outer room where Shirley was leaning over her copy of *The Iliad*.

"How's the Trojan War going?" I asked and took a seat in front of her desk.

"About the same every time I read it. Hector's a prince, and Achilles is a heel." She chuckled at her own choice of words. "No pun intended."

"Good one." I laughed out loud. "That's the way I remember it, too."

"You like *The Iliad*?" Her eyes lit up.

"I was an English major. That book was the first ancient text I read, and I was captivated by it," I said.

"You've read it more than once, then?" Shirley asked.

"Yes. I'm like you. I read it every now and then. Even though it's gory and violent, the story is fascinating and teaches us a lot about pride and vanity."

"Imagine all those men dying because one guy ran off with a pretty woman," Shirley said.

I told Shirley about my conversation with Buck and Archie and how they said men do stupid things when a woman is involved. "By the way," I said and tried to make it sound like an innocent question. "Do you know Veronica Bradwell?"

Shirley raised one eyebrow. "Yes. I know who she is. Why are you asking about her?"

"She showed up at my uncle's place yesterday and she seems to take quite an interest in him."

"Is that right? What kind of interest?"

"I'd say the romantic kind," I said. "Can you tell me anything about her? She didn't seem like she was from this part of the country."

Shirley leaned back in her chair and folded her hands in her lap. "Mrs. Bradwell moved here a year or so ago. Seems she inherited a house in town and a few acres east of here."

"What do you think of her?"

Shirley shrugged. "She seems nice enough. She stopped by

here to say hello not long after she moved in. She sidled up to Ruddy, telling him he was about the handsomest man she'd ever seen."

Laugh lines deepened around Shirley's eyes. "But when he started asking her questions about where she came from, she skedaddled pretty fast." Shirley laughed. "Ruddy's not exactly an expert on the social graces, you know. He thinks giving somebody the third degree is being neighborly, and my impression was Mrs. Bradwell didn't want to share her past history with us."

Chapter 27

Pastor John Arrives

I spent Monday afternoon packing a few things to drive to Balmoral County the following day to begin our hunt for Sinclair. When the doorbell rang, I had a bad feeling it was Ronnie coming back to fawn all over Uncle Charlie again. Frank had returned to the sheriff's office to file some paperwork, so Greg stood behind me as I answered the door.

The man on the porch was big. Real big. He had dark hair and a full beard. I could feel Greg tense as he stepped up beside me, and I knew he was ready to pull the Glock.

The screen door was locked as usual, and I spoke through it. "Yes?"

The man took off his red baseball cap and nodded. "Is this the home of Charles Deakin?" he asked.

Greg's hand inched inside his jacket, and his voice had a harsh, metallic sound to it. "Who are you?"

The man's eyebrows knitted together when he heard Greg's tone. "My name is John Nasmyth. I'm a friend of Sinclair Alderson's. He told me he was coming to visit his army pal and gave me this address." He paused, obviously surprised by the less-than-hospitable welcome. "I'm sorry if I'm intruding. I haven't been able to reach Sinclair, and I'm concerned about him."

Although the man's bulk was imposing, his voice was low and gentle. I looked beyond him and saw a white camper. "We'd like to see some identification, please," I said. My voice sounded thin and tinny, probably the result of the fear that was pulsing through me. I had been a deputy for just a few hours, and I was already regretting it.

John Nasmyth's left hand started to move toward his back pocket, but I saw his eyes land on the bulge in Greg's jacket. He stopped and held both hands up. "I want you to know I'm not armed. I'm just going to get my wallet." He slowly retrieved the wallet from his back pocket, took out his driver's license, and held it up so we could read it. JOHN NASMYTH. ANCHORAGE AK.

There was a rustling noise behind us and Uncle Charlie limped into view. He squinted at the man through the screen. "What do your friends call you?" he asked.

The man's eyebrows shot up. "They call me Pastor John."

"And what does it say in the book of John, Chapter eight, Verse thirty-two, Pastor John?"

The big man smiled. "You will know the truth, and the truth will set you free."

Uncle Charlie took a step back. "Open the door, Cassie. This man did more for Sinclair in one meeting than all the rest of us did in a lifetime."

Sitting in one of the easy chairs with a mug of Dolly's extra dark roast coffee in front of him, Pastor John seemed to relax. "I guess I'm not the meekest looking guy around," he said, "but I never got the third degree while doing a house visit before."

"And you probably never had a body search either, but we have to be careful," Greg said.

Pastor John nodded. "I understand that."

Uncle Charlie leaned toward the newcomer. "Sinclair told me about how you found him and brought him to your home. That was a good deed you did for him. It turned him around."

"I was deeply moved by Sinclair's guilt over his sister's death. When I dropped him off at his trailer, I thought God had started him on the road to recovery so he'd be able to deal with his sorrow in a positive way. I thought he was coming to see you as a first step in his journey." He shook his head in disbelief. "But he didn't tell me he had some kind of evidence about his sister's death."

"Sinclair told me he found it in his sister's Bible after he talked to you."

Pastor John shook his head. He looked at me. "Do you suppose the note he found is really important?"

Preachers make me nervous. I assume they know so much more than I do, and I'm sure they have a closer connection to the Almighty. As much as I hated my growing reputation for being the skeptical one, I didn't want to give hope to this man. "I think Sinclair was grasping at straws. He found something in his sister's Bible, and he just assumed it was an answer to his prayer."

"Could be," Pastor John replied. "It's just that I do believe in the power of prayer, Cassie. But I also know people can misread the situation, and I regret anything I may have done that would have caused Sinclair to go off tilting at windmills."

"And you came all the way here from Alaska to help him?" My voice was heavy with disbelief.

"Not exactly. I have relatives in Utah, and I've promised for years that I'd visit them, so I flew down there and stayed for a couple of days. But the whole time I was there, I felt something telling me to find Sinclair, so I borrowed my nephew's camper and drove here."

"I've been trying to contact Sinclair also," Uncle Charlie said. "The authorities think the robbers must have thought there was something valuable in that box."

"Do they know who the thieves were?" Pastor John asked.

"Ex-cons." Frank's voice broke through, and we all jumped. He had come in the back door while we were talking and had been quietly observing us from the kitchen, evaluating who this Pastor John was.

Uncle Charlie introduced them and explained the situation. Frank looked satisfied that John was legitimate. He sat on the couch next to Uncle Charlie and handed him a legal-size paper. "The fingerprint analysis came back. Here's the report."

"So Shorty did time for theft." Uncle Charlie flipped the page over. "And Muscle Man was in for manslaughter?"

"Right." Frank looked over Uncle's shoulder. "They were both in the state pen at the same time. Probably became friends there. Both of them got out early for good behavior."

Greg snorted. "I don't believe those two knew anything about good behavior."

"Does anybody know where they got the idea there was something valuable in Charlie's barn?" Pastor John asked.

"Nope. Ruddy sent somebody over to interview the parole board and some of the other inmates, but so far it's a no-go. He's asked me to try to find Sinclair."

"And me," I said and tossed my head.

"I don't like you being involved, Cassie," Uncle Charlie said.

I opened my jacket and flashed the deputy badge. "Sheriff Buchanan thinks I can help Frank." I decided against getting sarcastic. I wanted Uncle to understand I was doing this to get to the bottom of it all.

Pastor John took a last swallow of coffee. "I want to help. I feel responsible for what's happened."

"I'll have to clear that with Sheriff Buchanan," Frank said. I was pretty sure he could make that decision on his own, but I thought he might be buying time to think about taking this stranger along with us when we drove over to Balmoral County. "Cassie and I are leaving tomorrow morning to go to Balmoral County. If necessary, we'll continue on to Willard County to see if we can get a bead on Sinclair."

Uncle Charlie sat forward. "I want to go too."

"Not you, Charlie," Frank said. "You're still injured, and you might slow us down. You stay here with Dolly and Greg, and we'll call you as soon as we get something."

Pastor John stood. "I have a camper outside. I'll find a campsite nearby and spend the night." He gave Frank his phone number. "Text me whatever your decision is." He looked down at his hands, then back at Frank. "Just know this. Whether or not you want me on your team, I'm going to be looking for Sinclair. I have a sense inside that this is something God wants me to do."

"All right," Frank said. "I'll let you know."

After Pastor John left, we huddled around the table. "What do you think?" Frank asked. "Should we include the minister or not?"

"I vote yes," Uncle Charlie said. "He verified everything Sinclair told me about their meeting, and I don't think he has any bad intentions."

"Cassie?" Frank looked over at me.

"I vote yes. Not because I trust him, but I'd rather have him with us than leave him here with Uncle Charlie."

Greg and Dolly both added their agreement.

"Then it's settled." Frank took his phone out to text Pastor John. "We'll take him with us on our hunt for Sinclair."

I reached over and put my hand on Uncle's shoulder. "We won't let you down."

Chapter 28

Frank's Past

I was still thinking about what Pastor John said as I went out to bring the horses into the barn. Greg followed me and caught up before I got to the gate of the corral.

"Cassie, do you have a minute to talk?" His voice had a serious ring to it, and the scar stood out white against his pale skin.

"Sure," I said. I figured he was going to ask me about Dolly. The way they had been looking at each other, I had a feeling they were jumpstarting a serious relationship.

But Greg surprised me. "There's something I've been meaning to talk to you about." He glanced back at the house, then pointed to the barn. "Let's talk behind the barn so we won't get interrupted again."

That seemed a little overly cautious to me, but I'd gotten used to the strange and secretive ways of law enforcement, so we walked behind the barn. I sat on a bale of straw while Greg stood in front of me and ran his hand through his strawberry hair.

I never took Greg to be one of those people who was going to tell me what was wrong with my life, but this looked like lecture time. I pulled my legs up onto the bale and sat cross-legged with my back against the barn. I sighed with enough emphasis so he would get it.

"Cassie, I don't like to insert myself into other people's personal lives."

Any time you hear somebody say they don't like to insert themselves into other people's personal lives, it's a sure bet they're getting ready to insert themselves right into the middle of yours. Big time. I unfolded myself and moved to stand up. "That's a good philosophy to have, Greg. Maybe you should follow it now."

He put a hand on my shoulder. "Just hear me out, Cassie. Before you and Frank take off together in search of Sinclair, there's something I want to tell you about Frank."

Now this sounded promising. I sat back down. "Let me guess. You're going to tell me that Frank can't be trusted."

Greg looked at me with wide eyes. "Where in the world did you get that idea?"

I shrugged. "I think lying comes easy to Frank. I don't think I can trust him."

"Cassie, you're way off the mark. Frank is the most honest and dedicated lawman I've ever known."

"But you said you didn't like being his partner."

"No. I said being Frank's partner put me in danger because of the job we were doing. It didn't have anything to do with Frank himself." He pressed his lips together. "I wanted to explain to you why Frank is so determined to hunt down criminals and why he has trouble with relationships."

"That's a lot to explain before I have to take the horses in." My talent for sarcasm was making an entrance, but I couldn't help it.

Greg sighed. "I'll keep it short. Frank's father was a police detective in Kentucky. He was a hard worker and well-known for being effective. Frank was an only child, and the family was close. When Frank was in college, studying to be an aerospace engineer, something terrible happened."

"Frank wanted to be an aerospace engineer?" I felt a little shift inside of me, like a piece of a puzzle had dropped into place. I remembered the way Frank's eyes lit up once when we were talking about the physics of flight. "What happened?" I asked. "Did he flunk out of school?"

"No. Nothing like that. You know how focused he is. He probably aced every test he ever took."

"What, then?"

The scar on Greg's face changed shape as he clenched his teeth. "Frank's parents were out at dinner one night when a man approached their table with a gun. Witnesses said Frank's father was very calm and tried to talk the man into putting the gun down."

I sat still, knowing this would not end well.

"He shot Frank's father at point-blank range. When his mother bent over her dying husband, the man shot her. They both died at the scene."

I felt like I'd been punched. I had been acting like a spoiled brat for days, telling Frank he didn't know how it felt to be alone and questioning his honesty. My voice came out in a whisper. "Did they catch the man who did that?"

"No. They have a security video of him, but it's grainy, and no one knows for sure who he was." Greg sighed. "Frank told me he decided on a career in law enforcement after his parents were murdered."

"A personal vendetta?"

"No. He just wants to help clean up society. He doesn't want anyone else to suffer a cruel death like that. And he wants to protect children from losing their parents." Greg looked around to make sure no one was close and dropped his voice even lower. "Frank won't admit it, but I think he wants to find the man who killed his parents. I don't know how he plans to do that, but Frank's a pretty resourceful guy. I wouldn't put anything past him. That may be why he left DEA and came here."

"Wow." I stood.

Greg's ginger-colored brows furrowed. "Frank confided in me that he won't get into a serious relationship with anyone because he thinks that puts them in danger. Like his mother being killed because she was married to his father."

I let it all sink in. Frank's getting close and then backing away. That combination of desire mixed with reluctance. I felt like banging my head against the side of the barn for being so stupid. And so rude.

Greg took me by the shoulders. "Don't tell Frank I told you all this. He's a real private person, and he won't like it."

"I won't." I put my arms around Greg's waist and hugged him hard. "Thanks."

We were standing there like that, hugging each other and lost in the sadness of it all when we heard footsteps and turned to see Frank rounding the side of the barn. Greg and I quickly stepped apart, and the three of us stared at each other in silence.

"Sorry," Frank said. "I thought you might need some help with the horses." He turned away. "I guess I was wrong."

Chapter 29

Balmoral County

The dust was already swirling at eight o'clock in the morning as Frank, Pastor John, and I climbed into the Explorer. Uncle Charlie, Greg, and Dolly stood on the porch and waved goodbye as we headed south to Balmoral County. The dirt road that led away from Uncle Charlie's farm rose up behind the Explorer until the farmhouse faded away. I shook off the feeling that it was a kind of omen and looked forward.

I had opted for the back seat so that Frank and Pastor John could get acquainted while I checked maps of the area we were headed to. Turned out Pastor John had been a helicopter pilot in Vietnam. While he explained the complexities of flying a Huey in the midst of combat, I reviewed the topography.

We were heading to a higher elevation, a part of the country where farms lay among forests, rivers, and hills. Balmoral was a big county, and according to what Uncle Charlie could remember, Sinclair's parents' farm lay on the eastern edge. But the sheriff's office was in the west, closer to our own trajectory.

We passed a McDonald's in a small town on the way and

stopped for coffee and a snack to hold us over, and we got to the sheriff's office in Claxon just before ten a.m.

The building spoke of plain living. Nothing fancy about the cedar siding that was painted brown and matched the pines in the center of the town square. The other buildings around the square showed the same lack of flair, and I wondered if they only had one paint color at the local Sherwin-Williams store.

But inside, the walls of the office were a light ivory. A middle-aged woman sat behind a desk in the front office. With hairspray-tamed hair and red nail polish, she was quite a departure from the rough-and-tumble Shirley. "Can I help you?" she asked politely.

Frank showed her his badge and asked to see Sheriff Easterly.

"Yes, Sheriff Easterly is expecting you." She lifted the receiver on her phone and punched a button. "Deputy White is here," she said. "He has two people with him." She pointed us toward a door to the right, which opened as soon as we moved toward it.

I was a little surprised when Sheriff Easterly walked out. He was a small, wiry man, not the Gary Cooper kind of guy I had come to picture in all western towns.

"I'm Ryan Easterly," he said as he offered his hand. His voice had a kind of high, whiny pitch to it, and his face came to a point at the end of a nose that reminded me of a weasel. His small, dark eyes behind rimless glasses darted back and forth among us as we shook hands. He wasn't even wearing cowboy boots.

He ushered us into his office and motioned to chairs in front of the desk. He didn't look like a man who would be comfortable with small talk, and he proved it with an abrupt beginning to the meeting. "What can I do for you?"

Frank began. "Thank you for seeing us, Sheriff Easterly. As you know, we're looking for Sinclair Alderson, and we understand he met with you recently. We've been trying to contact him, but haven't been successful so far."

Easterly sat straight in his chair with his arms at his side. He looked uncomfortable. "Yes, Mr. Alderson came here a few days ago. Hold on, I'll check when that was." He picked up the telephone and hit a button. "Millie, when did that fella Sinclair come by to see me?" There was a pause as he rapped his fingertips on the desk. "Tuesday? Okay. Thanks."

He dropped the receiver back in the cradle. "It was last Tuesday afternoon. He came in and told me he wanted to reopen an old investigation. His sister died forty years ago, and Mr. Alderson thought it wasn't an accident." He cleared his throat. "I told him I wasn't the sheriff then. That was Sheriff Sunderman."

"Where is Sheriff Sunderman now?" I asked.

"He died a little over a year ago."

"And you became sheriff then?" Frank asked.

"Yes. It was the darnedest thing." He seemed to get more comfortable as he settled into his background. "I moved out here from the east coast after my wife and I broke up. I needed a new start, and I was glad to get out of the city and become a deputy in a rural area. When I got here, Sunderman was sheriff and there was one other deputy who had seniority over me, so I figured I could ride out my time to retirement with a quiet position as low man on the totem pole. You know, get sent out for coffee and that kind of thing, but it didn't work out that way. After Sunderman died, the other fella quit and left me holding the bag."

"Why did he quit?"

"He moved to New Mexico and took a job in construction. Said he'd rather be building things than chasing criminals. I think the idea of being in charge scared him. All of a sudden, I found myself sitting behind this desk." He knocked on the wood with his knuckles. "I don't mind telling you, I thought about quitting right then, but it didn't seem right to leave the folks here high and dry, so I decided to hang on until we could get somebody in." He sighed. "Six months ago, they put me on the ballot and elected me their sheriff. Said I was doing a fine job." He shook his head. "I'm still getting my feet on the ground, but luckily we haven't had any big problems."

"Glad you decided to stay," Frank said. "It's getting hard to find good people in law enforcement."

"Well, I'm doing the best I can," Easterly said. "On the scale of western sheriffs, I probably don't amount to much. Even my name works against me." He pointed to the nameplate on the front of his desk and chuckled. "Folks like to tease me about it, but they don't mean any real harm."

"I'm sure they're glad to have you," Frank said.

"I don't know how glad they are, but they're stuck with me for now, and they've been real supportive." He paused and scratched at the side of his face. "To be honest, I think they're afraid I might leave, and then one of them would have to step up to the plate."

I liked this man, and I believed him when he said he was trying to do the right thing, but Frank's words hung in my mind. You don't know who you can trust.

"You wanted to hear about Mr. Alderson." Easterly stood, went to a file cabinet in the corner, and pulled out a manila folder. "When he stopped in, I looked up his sister's case in our system and saw that Lacey Alderson was an eight-year-old girl who died in 1970 from a fall off the side of a cliff in the Piedmont area of the county." He looked at me. "That's the eastern half, where there's a high precipice next to a river."

"Is that the official report?" Frank asked.

"Yes. It's a copy of the official report on the case." He read from the first page. "It was determined that Lacey Alderson fell off the side of a sheer cliff in a patch of woods behind the Alderson farm on August 12, 1970. It is believed she died in the fall. One of the child's shoes was found on the side of the cliff. Her body landed in the Flagon River and was carried downstream. A group of hikers discovered it that afternoon."

He looked up. "It's a pretty cut-and-dry case. There were no signs of a struggle and no indication that she had been sexually assaulted." He flipped a page on the report. "According to the parents, Lacey frequently played in that area, although the mother said she never went near that cliff."

I glanced at Frank. That's exactly what Sinclair had said. "Did Mr. Alderson say he had any new evidence?" I asked.

"No. He didn't say anything about new evidence, but then that may be because I told him I wasn't sure I had the authority to reopen the case."

Frank raised his eyebrows.

Easterly tapped the page in front of him. "The investigation wasn't handled by the Balmoral County sheriff's office."

"Why not?" Frank asked.

"Because the child's body had washed downriver and was discovered in Willard County. Therefore, that office was in charge."

"Who was the sheriff there?" Frank asked.

"Sheriff Mannie Jessop."

"Is he still around?" Pastor John asked.

"His son, Bob Jessop, is sheriff now. I called him and arranged for Mr. Alderson to drive over there."

"Did Sheriff Sunderman consult with the other sheriff on the case?" I asked.

Easterly ran his finger down the page. "Sheriff Sunderman made a hand-written note here that he was working another case at the time and wasn't as involved in this one as he might have been."

That caught my attention. "Another death?" I asked.

"No." Easterly adjusted his glasses. "Sunderman wrote here that a girl had been reported missing, but it was believed she was a runaway."

"Did he say who the runaway was?" Frank asked. "Did he find her?"

Easterly's eyes followed his fingers down the page. "The girl's name was Jane Satterfield. I looked up that case too." He gestured toward the file cabinet. "They never located her, but they found some of her belongings at a truck stop about fifty miles east of here. Sheriff Sunderman left the case open, but marked it as a likely runaway." He put the file folder down on his desk. "That's about all I have. I'll get Millie to make a copy of this report for you if you like. And I'll call Jessop if you want to meet with him."

"I've already made arrangements to meet with Bob Jessop," Frank said. "But if his father is still around, I'd like to talk to him as well."

While Millie made a copy of the report, Easterly phoned and let Sheriff Jessop know we would be driving over within an hour.

Easterly walked us out to the car. "I wish I could help more," he said.

"What did you think of Sinclair Alderson?" Pastor John asked. "What was his state of mind?"

Easterly rubbed his chin. "He seemed disappointed that I couldn't help him, but he was real polite. I asked him to keep me informed, and he said he would."

"Did you hear from him again? Did he phone or stop by?" Frank asked.

"No. He left late Tuesday afternoon, and I didn't see or hear from him again."

We all thanked him. The air was hot and dusty, and my mouth was as dried-up as sawdust. "Is it always this dry around here?" I asked.

Easterly nodded thoughtfully. "This area's been in a drought for decades. Some of the farmers have given up and gone away." He shook our hands again, waved, and returned inside the building.

I leaned against the side of the Explorer, sipping from my

water bottle. Pastor John toed the dirt with his boot and frowned while Frank called Uncle Charlie to see if he'd heard anything.

"Not much information here," I heard Frank say. "We're heading to Willard County to talk to the sheriff there. We'll check in later." He clicked off and turned to us. "Charlie still hasn't heard from Sinclair. What do you think, Cassie?"

"As far as finding Sinclair, I think we're kinestatic."

"What does that mean?" Frank asked.

"We're putting in lots of miles, but we may not be getting anywhere."

"Good word," Frank said. "It explains a lot about detective work." He opened the car door for me. "Let's put in a few more miles."

Chapter 30

Willard County

Frank opened the GPS app on his phone, and we all looked at the distance to Willard County. "If it's all right with you two," Frank said, "let's talk to Sheriff Jessop before we have lunch."

That suited Pastor John and me just fine. We were all eager to get to Willard County. Maybe they would have a clue to Sinclair's whereabouts.

The counties in that area of the country were all odd-shaped. We had driven south to get to Easterly's office. Now we headed mostly southeast to get to Willard County. If we didn't find Sinclair by the time we met with the sheriff there, the plan was to go back up to the eastern edge of Balmoral County and find the farm that Sinclair's parents had owned.

I tried to nap in the back seat of the Explorer while the men talked quietly, but my brain kept reviewing what Sheriff Easterly had said. There wasn't much there to pin a hope on.

We found the sheriff's office in Willard County without any problem. It was a little building made out of concrete blocks.

Sturdy as they come. Clearly, a no-nonsense kind of place. It was on the edge of Prescott, a town with a main street and little else. I spotted the post office and a drugstore. I guessed the folks in Prescott traveled elsewhere for their groceries.

There was a gravel area in front of the building with a sheriff's cruiser and a pickup truck parked there. We pulled up beside the cruiser.

It was already early afternoon. The sun was hot, my throat was still dry, and it was looking more and more like this was an exercise in futility. Frank was frowning, but Pastor John seemed to have only one expression, and that was one of serenity.

There was no receptionist in the Willard County Sheriff's Office. By the size of things, I guessed there were no funds to add another person. The outer room had a desk with a pleasant-looking man sitting behind it. The name sign on the front of the desk read "Sheriff Bob Jessop."

He looked up when we entered and put his phone on the desk. I wondered what apps a sheriff had on his phone. "Can I help you?" he asked politely.

Jessop was one of those people it was hard to pin an age on. He was slender and tanned, with a boyish face and sandy-colored hair that was thinning. I guessed forties or maybe a young-looking fifties. He flashed a gorgeous smile that made me think he'd be a good model for Esquire, and I wondered why he chose small-town law enforcement for a career.

Frank introduced us and we shook hands all around. "You wanted to talk about Mr. Alderson?" Jessop said.

"That's right," Frank said. "We understand he stopped by to talk to you about his sister's death."

"He was here last week. While he and I were talking, I got a call to check on a domestic violence situation, and I had to leave. My dad was here, though, and he finished interviewing Mr. Alderson. Do you want to talk to him?"

"Please," Frank said.

Jessop walked out of the office and opened another door. I heard him call, "Hey Dad. The deputy from Buchanan's office is here."

While we waited, I scanned the pictures and citations that lined the walls of the office. More than a few of them showed an older man standing next to a young Bob Jessop. I assumed the older man was Bob's father. The largest photo showed the two of them standing behind a pickup truck with expressions of masculine delight on their faces and a large, dead elk lying at their feet.

When Jessop returned, he was followed by a taller, more muscular man. Bob Jessop introduced him. "This is my father, Sheriff Mannie Jessop. I took over when he retired."

I recognized him as the man in the picture. His hair had more gray in it, but he still looked fit. Another Gary Cooper western look-alike, but with a few extra years on him.

"Glad to meet you," the elder Jessop said. He had a strong voice and a nice smile, and he shook each of our hands vigorously. When I introduced myself, his smile got wider. "Good to see a young woman in law enforcement," he said. "We need more of the gentler sex, especially out here in the wild west."

If I had to pick a word to describe him, I would have said "genial." He looked like a man who had paid his dues and was relaxed and happy in his old stomping grounds.

"It must be a source of pride to you that your son has kept your legacy going," I said.

"It sure is. When I retired, the good people of Willard County voted Bob in as sheriff." The elder Jessop rocked back on his heels, paternal pride glowing on his face. "I can't tell you how proud I am. This young man is a better sheriff than I ever was."

"Don't believe a word of it," Bob Jessop said. "My dad is a legend in this county. Best sheriff ever."

"Sounds like a mutual admiration society," I said.

Mannie gave a sharp nod of his head. "Yep. That's exactly what it is." He looked over at Bob. "There's just about nothin' better for a man than having a good son."

"Looks like you've both been busy," Frank said. "That's an impressive array of citations and photos."

"You have to blame my wife for those," Mannie said. "She's always trying to pretty up the place."

"That's a wonderful photo." I pointed to the large picture on the wall that I had been studying.

"Ah, yes." Mannie walked to my side. "I took Bob on a hunting trip for his eighteenth birthday, and he bagged that twelve-point bull elk all on his own." He nodded toward the picture. "Those antlers are hanging above my fireplace at home."

We all gathered around to admire the Jessops' hunting expertise. I didn't mention that I hate seeing dead animals.

"Well done," Frank said.

"Yep. It was a day to remember." Mannie Jessop walked to the other side of the room and lowered himself into one of the chairs. I noticed scuffs on his cowboy boots. He must still enjoy the outdoors.

"Sheriff Jessop," Frank said and took a seat next to Mannie. "I understand you were here when Sinclair Alderson came by last week to discuss his sister's death."

"That's right." Mannie Jessop turned toward his son. "When did he stop by, Bob?"

"Last Wednesday. Remember, I got called away to the Baylors' farm. Jimmy and Caroline were going at it again."

"Oh yeah. Wednesday." Mannie turned back to Frank. "My memory isn't what it used to be," he said, "but I sure remember the meeting I had with Mr. Alderson."

"Tell us about it," Frank said.

"Alderson wanted to talk about his sister's death. He said he came across something recently that made him think her death wasn't an accident, and he wanted us to review the case. I got the file out and went over it with him." He gestured toward the door leading to the hall. "I have the report back in the file room if you want to see it."

"Thanks," Frank said. "We got a copy from Sheriff Easterly. Can you tell us anything about the incident? We understand you were the officer in charge of the investigation."

Mannie Jessop took a deep breath and rubbed the back of his neck. "It was a long time ago, but it's the kind of thing you don't forget. A little child like that. Some hikers found her body in the river. It flows just a mile or so from here. They pulled her out of the water, and one of them came over here to report it." He shook his head. "I was on duty at the time, so I went back with them. You don't ever want to see something like that."

"How long had the child been dead?" Frank asked.

"Not long. The coroner ruled she had died within about six hours of when she was found. Of course, the water makes a difference. They found her in the late afternoon. Her parents hadn't even missed her. One of the hikers recognized her, and we rode right over to ask them to come to the morgue to identify the body."

"That must have been terrible," I said.

He clenched his teeth and stared off into space. "Worse than terrible."

"So, you ruled it was an accidental death?" Frank asked.

"Yes. There were no indications of a struggle, and she hadn't been sexually assaulted. Her parents said she really didn't have any friends, living way out in the country like they did. When we found her shoe over on the side of that cliff behind her parents' home, we realized she must have fallen to her death. A couple of bruises on her head and shoulder seemed to verify that."

"Thanks for giving us your personal recollection," Frank said. "How did your meeting with Sinclair Alderson go?"

Mannie Jessop took another deep breath and sighed. "You may

not know this, but I had met Mr. Alderson before. He came to see me after he got out of the army and found out his sister had died. That was thirty-nine years ago. He was convinced back then that it wasn't an accident, but this time he said he had proof."

"Did he show you what proof he had?" I asked.

"No." He clasped his hands together. "To be honest, I could smell alcohol on his breath, and I thought he was just making it up." He looked at me. "People do that sometimes when they don't want to admit that an accident can take away a loved one."

"You noticed alcohol on his breath?" Pastor John asked. "Are you sure?"

Mannie Jessop's blue eyes turned dark. "When you've been a sheriff as long as I have, Mr. Nasmyth, you get real good at detecting the odor of alcohol." He shook his head. "Booze causes more trouble than just about anything else."

"Did Sinclair say anything that could help us find him?" I asked.

"No." Mannie Jessop bit on his bottom lip. "But he told me something that made me think he'd gone off the deep end."

"What was that?" Frank asked.

"He said he had stopped at a campsite the night before and met some bikers who said they were on a Christian mission to spread the Word. He said he shared his story about his sister with them and told them he had left something valuable with a friend of his. They said they would pray for him."

"Did he tell you what the valuable thing was or who he left it with?" I asked.

"No. I asked him point blank, but by that time he was getting agitated." Jessop frowned. "That's when I decided the guy had gone nuts. No sane person would share information like that with a bunch of strangers, no matter how many hymns they were singing.

"I guess he was just plain desperate. We get that sometimes when somebody wants us to reopen an investigation. I think this Sinclair fella wanted to believe his sister was killed, and he didn't care what the facts were." He raised his hands, palms out. "I felt sorry for him. I told him I'd look into it personally, but I couldn't promise anything."

"How did he take that?" Frank asked.

"He got mad. Said I wasn't doing my job. By that time, I started to worry that he was going to do something crazy. He stomped out of here, saying he was going to prove me wrong." He dropped his hands back on the arms of his chair. "To be honest, I was glad to see him go. I hoped he might go off somewhere and sober up."

We got up to leave, and Mannie Jessop walked us to the door.

"By the way," Frank said, "Sheriff Easterly said there was another case that was being handled at the same time. The previous sheriff was trying to find a teenage girl runaway. Do you know anything about that?"

Mannie Jessop rubbed his chin. "I remember Sunderman saying he was looking for somebody, but I was pretty tied up with the Alderson girl's death. I don't know what happened in that runaway case."

"Well, thanks." Frank tipped his baseball cap, and we left the office.

The three of us stood in the parking lot between the Explorer and the sheriff's cruiser. "What do you think?" Frank asked.

"I'm troubled about the alcohol," Pastor John said.

Frank looked at me. "Cassie?"

"I'm confused," I said. "Sheriff Easterly described Sinclair as determined, but polite. But Sheriff Jessop says he was agitated and aggressive."

"It makes sense to me," Frank said. "Easterly couldn't help

because it wasn't in his jurisdiction, so Sinclair was pinning all his hopes on Sheriff Jessop. When that didn't work, Sinclair got mad."

I looked at Pastor John, hoping he might have some insight, but he was staring off into the distance, lost in thought.

Chapter 31

Shoalton

Pastor John chose the back seat for our ride to the Alderson farm. He said he wanted to read Scripture and pray, so I took shotgun while Frank drove.

"Any more ideas?" Frank asked me as we headed back to Balmoral County.

"I guess we know how those thieves got information about Sinclair's box," I said. "Sinclair sounds like an idiot. If he convinced those bikers there was something of real value in Uncle Charlie's barn, then the only explanation is that some of those bikers decided to steal it. If that's what happened, then Sinclair is the reason Uncle Charlie got injured." I could feel the heat rising in my face. I wanted to get my hands on Sinclair and shake him until his teeth fell out.

"I hate to say it, but I'm afraid Cassie may be right," Pastor John said. "It happens sometimes to new believers. I'm afraid Sinclair was taken in by people who pretended to be Christians, but they weren't."

"Like Frank keeps reminding me," I said, "you can't trust anybody."

I turned in my seat to look at Pastor John. He claimed to be a believer, but what did we really know about him? He knew Scripture. That was for real. But why was he so interested? Was there more to Sinclair's life than we knew? Did Pastor John really care about a madman claiming his sister was murdered?

"Something isn't right," I said out loud. Sinclair was a man on a mission, determined to find out what happened to his sister. In addition, he believed he had "found God" as he told Uncle Charlie. Why would he just fall off the face of the earth and go silent? Why wouldn't he stay in contact with Charlie or Pastor John? But then, Sheriff Jessop said he had smelled alcohol on Sinclair's breath. He was probably drinking again. Maybe he was in a ditch somewhere, sleeping it off.

Frank reached over and touched my shoulder. "Hey. Didn't you hear me?"

I realized I had been in what my dad used to call "Cassie Zone." I could get so focused inside my own head, I wouldn't hear what was going on around me. "Sorry. I was just thinking about this whole crazy situation."

"You said you thought something wasn't right. Tell me what you're thinking."

"Uncle Charlie said Sinclair called him Wednesday and left a message. Why didn't Sinclair call back later if he wanted to talk about the case?"

"I think it's clear. He wasn't getting any encouragement that they would reopen the case, and he must have known the note he found wouldn't help." He tapped on the steering wheel with his finger. "Maybe he just didn't want to admit to Charlie that he was wrong about the whole thing." He glanced at me. "Add the alcohol in, and who knows what Sinclair might do."

"I guess so." I leaned my head back against the headrest and watched the drought-stricken landscape slide by the passenger window. My thoughts turned from Sinclair to his little sister.

What had it been like for a child to grow up here in the middle of nowhere? From what I had learned about Lacey Alderson, she found her happiness in the nature around her.

When I was growing up, my dad's house was on a small street with just a few other houses. Mr. and Mrs. Oliver lived in one of the homes that had a little patch of woods behind it, and my friends and I used to go there to play. We'd swing from the branches or play hide-and-seek. Sometimes we would race up and down the back alleys.

But to have all this open space. I wondered if a little kid might feel lost.

We drove on past the farms that made up that part of the county and we crossed over into Balmoral County again. The landscape was beginning to feel familiar.

The sign that announced Shoalton pointed right. "This is the turn," Frank said.

Uncle Charlie had told us Sinclair's place was outside Shoalton. "We'll have to find somebody who can give us directions," I said. "Google Maps doesn't recognize the Alderson farm."

The road turned into a smaller two-lane county road that hadn't had much work done on it in a while, but then I didn't think it got much traffic.

We rolled into a town about the size of a matchbox and Frank stopped in front of the Shoalton Cafe. "How about this place for lunch?" he asked.

"Looks good to me," I said, and Pastor John nodded his approval.

Frank released his seat belt. "Maybe somebody here can give us directions to the Alderson farm."

We piled out and trooped into the little cafe. Inside it was warm, and I smelled hamburgers on the grill. Once again, I was surprised at how hungry I was. We stepped up to the bar to order.

The man who waited on us had a broad, likable face, and he

was wearing one of those white paper hats. We all wanted hamburgers and fries. He wrote it down and slid the order over a counter to the cook. "Strangers, eh?" he asked.

"Yeah," Frank replied. "How can you tell?"

"I guess I know everybody in this little town," he said. "At least everybody who comes in here to eat—and that's pretty much everybody in town." His face broke into a toothy smile, and he held his hand out to Frank. "I'm Jake. This is my place."

Frank shook hands. "Frank White." He didn't show his badge. "This is Cassie and Pastor John. We're looking for a friend who used to live in these parts. We think he came back through here recently."

"Oh?" Jake wiped the bar with his towel. "What's your friend's name?"

"Sinclair Alderson."

"If he came through, he didn't stop here," Jake said. "You're the first strangers I've seen in a couple of weeks."

"His family used to own a farm around here," Frank said. "Ever hear of the Alderson farm?"

Jake stopped his wiping. "Sounds vaguely familiar, but I'm not originally from this area. My wife and I moved here fifteen years ago. I bet Ms. McCochran would know, though."

"Who's Ms. McCochran?" I asked.

"She's one of the ladies who bakes the pies and bread we sell here. She's been around forever and knows just about every detail there is to know about this place." He looked at his watch. "She'll be in soon to deliver some baked goods."

We sat at a table in the corner, and Jake brought our food. It was standard burger and fries, but it was very good, and I gobbled it down like it was five-star cuisine.

We were finishing up when a tall woman wearing a white T-shirt and dark blue polyester slacks came in the front door. Her legs were so long that the hem of her slacks was a couple of inches above her ankles.

"I've got those pies for you, Jake," she announced, and he came around to the front of the counter.

We saw him speak low to her and he gestured toward our table. She walked toward us. She looked to be in her eighties and was as straight as a ramrod. I could see the effects of a lifetime of hard work on her face and hands.

"Jake says you folks are looking for the Alderson farm," she said.

We all stood. "Yes ma'am," Frank said. "We're looking for Sinclair Alderson, and we were told he came back to see his parents' old place."

"Sinclair's here?" Her eyes widened. "I thought he moved to Canada."

"Actually, he was in Alaska," Pastor John said and held out his hand. "I'm his minister."

She eyed Pastor John, and I guess she was convinced because her face softened and she took his hand. "Well, I'll be," she said. "Sinclair Alderson. I haven't heard that name in decades." She looked back at Frank. "If you find him, tell him to come by to see the McCochran sisters. We knew him and his family a long time ago."

Jake had gone out to get the baked goods, and he came back in carrying a big box that I could see was loaded with pies. He put the box on the counter, took one of the pastries off the top, and placed it in the middle of our table. "You've got to have some of this. Ms. McCochran makes the best peach pie you've ever tasted." He removed the foil cover. "See the four-pointed star that's carved into the crust? That's her signature." He nodded toward Ms. McCochran. "Lois is famous in this town. Folks come in here asking for the star lady's pie."

Frank and I looked at each other over the pie. So Veronica

Bradwell was buying somebody else's pastries and claiming them as her own.

"I've got some business in town," Ms. McCochran said, "but if you wait a minute, I'll draw you a map that'll take you right out to the Alderson farm, though I don't expect Sinclair would get any warm feelings from seeing it. It's falling apart."

She walked behind the counter and got out a paper and pen.

Chapter 32

Finding Sinclair

Countdown to Sinclair. Our spirits lifted as we drove away from the Shoalton Cafe. We were full of good food, and we were on the final twenty-five miles to our destination.

Ms. McCochran had given us a lot of detail about what to expect. She said the place was in ruins. The rats had long since eaten whatever grain was in the barn, and there was nothing there but an occasional owl, but she thought all of those had left too. She said the whole area had a bad connotation because of Lacey's death.

Still, we believed Sinclair must have gone there within the past week. Maybe he decided to stay. At least we were getting closer to him.

Pastor John sat in the back seat again, and I could hear his quiet murmuring that I assumed were prayers. The way Frank gripped the steering wheel told me he saw the finish line in sight.

I had the directions Lois had written out, so I navigated as we drove out the state road we had come in on. "Turn left just past that big oak stump." The road narrowed into a path that looked like it hadn't known automobile tires for a long time. Weeds grew up in places that made the path almost a part of the surrounding grass.

The drought Sheriff Easterly told us about had withered the area to a desolate waste. As we drove farther, the vegetation disappeared. There was no life. Just dried-up berry bushes and an occasional tree that looked like it was hanging on for dear life. It all spoke of death, and I shivered even in the heat.

The clouds pulled themselves together into a dark mass that dropped a curtain of gloom all around, but no rain fell. It was eerie. Inside the Explorer, I felt the tension mount when I announced we were just a couple of miles from the homestead. We bumped along as the path got smaller and what was left of the weeds died away. The pathway took a turn to the left, and abruptly ended in a dirt-packed clearing. Frank pulled to a stop. Off to the right, about a hundred yards away, stood the house.

I suppose you'd call it a house. It was more like something out of a bad dream. A wooden shack with a small porch that had fallen down on one end. A single window was broken and one shard of glass still hung on. The front door was hanging off a couple of hinges.

To the left side of the house and a little behind it was a small barn. From what I could see, it had suffered the same indignities as the house. The barn doors were closed.

The sight of such devastation brought us all up short. Ms. McCochran's description of bad wasn't even close to the mark. Frank turned off the ignition, and we sat in silence.

I don't know exactly what I had expected. Maybe I wanted to see Sinclair in the front yard, chopping wood and making plans to rebuild. I envisioned him putting his ax down, wiping his brow, and giving a wave. Maybe a mongrel dog sitting by and looking up at Sinclair in admiration. But I didn't expect what I was seeing. The term "God-forsaken" came to mind.

"There's Sinclair's truck on the other side of the barn," Pastor John said and pointed. I heard him exhale a big breath. "He must be here."

We all got out and took a few steps. John led the way, his eagerness apparent in quick feet.

A horrible odor filled the air. "What's that smell?" I asked. "Is it a skunk?"

Frank stopped short. "John," he yelled. "Come here. Now." Pastor John looked back in surprise.

"*Now!*" Frank growled. John walked back toward us as Frank pulled his gun. "Cassie, get in the car."

"What?"

He grabbed my arm so hard it hurt and dragged me back to the Explorer, opened the door, and shoved me in the passenger seat. "Get your gun and wait here."

I opened the glove compartment and took out the .38. I checked the cylinder, locked it in place, and waited while Frank walked back to Pastor John.

They had a brief conference, bending toward each other while Frank talked. He pointed toward the house, and I watched the two of them move slowly in that direction. They pulled themselves up onto the porch and disappeared inside. I locked the doors to the Explorer. A sudden breeze rustled the spindly bushes that lined the side of the broad front yard, and I swiveled around in my seat. Nothing there.

It occurred to me that I was not equipped for this situation. Suppose Sinclair was in that house drinking himself into a stupor. What would I do if he killed Frank and Pastor John and came running out of the house toward the car? My nerves bristled, and a drop of sweat slid down the side of my face.

I had my eyes glued to the front of the house. I saw someone walk past the window, but it was so dark inside I couldn't make out who it was. Then Pastor John pushed the door aside and stepped onto the porch. His big bulk made the house look even smaller. But where was Frank? I held my breath. In a few seconds, Frank appeared, and I forced myself to exhale.

They both jumped down off the porch rather than risk the rotting steps. Frank said something to Pastor John and nodded toward the barn. I got out of the passenger door, but Frank motioned for me to get back in the car. The look on his face told me not to argue, so I slid back in the seat. My hand was sweaty around the handle of the .38.

Frank and John walked slowly toward the barn. Frank's gun was drawn. When they got to the door, they stopped, and I saw Frank motion for Pastor John to stand to the side. Frank put his hand on the door and swung it out quickly.

I couldn't see in the barn. It was too dark from where I was sitting, but I saw Frank stand completely still. Then he let his gun drop by his side, and he turned away. Pastor John moved around him to look in. Frank walked quickly back toward the car, but Pastor John stood as still as a statue, holding on to the door of the barn. I watched as he dropped to his knees and put his head in his hands. After a couple of seconds, he released his hands and his head turned toward the sky. He shouted "No!" so loud it made the hair on the back of my neck stand up.

I got out and stood frozen beside the car. Frank put his gun away and pulled his phone out of his pocket. With his phone propped against his ear, he grabbed my arm with his free hand. "Cassie, call your uncle."

Chapter 33

Bad News

The next few minutes felt as if they belonged in somebody else's life. While Frank talked to Sheriff Easterly on his phone, I called Uncle Charlie. Greg answered the phone, and I told him to put Uncle on the line so Frank could talk to him. While we waited, Frank got Pastor John back to the car.

"Put your phone on speaker," Frank told me. We stood beside the car. When Uncle came on the line, Frank cleared his throat. I saw the muscles in his jaw stand out. "Charlie," he said, "I have some bad news."

I could almost feel Uncle Charlie's anguish. He must have known what was coming. "Is it Sinclair?"

"Yes." Frank switched the phone to his other hand and rubbed his free hand on his jeans. "I'm sorry, but Sinclair is dead. It appears to be suicide."

I heard a sharp intake of breath from the phone. "How did it happen?"

"He hung himself in the barn next to his parents' old house."

Uncle Charlie's voice came across loud and intense. "Sinclair did not kill himself."

"I know you want to believe that, Charlie, but it's true."

"Trust me on this, Frank," Uncle Charlie said. "You're a good man, but you don't know Sinclair. He's the type of man who might kill somebody else if he got mad enough, but he'd never kill himself."

"He was depressed, Charlie. He had all this hope that he was going to find the truth about Lacey's death, but he just ran into one dead end after another. That'd be enough to take down any man."

"Not only would he not kill himself," Uncle Charlie said, "he certainly wouldn't hang himself. Sinclair couldn't tie his own shoelaces."

Frank and I looked at each other. "You're serious, Uncle Charlie?" I said.

"Listen, I know what I'm talking about. Frank, I want you to insist that there be an autopsy, and I want you to make sure nobody touches the rope that was used until I get there. Understand?"

"Yes, sir."

"Greg and I will drive over right now." There was a pause, and I could hear Greg say something in the background. Then Uncle Charlie got back on the line. "Dolly is coming with us. We don't want her to stay here alone. We may need directions, so keep your phone close by." There was a pause. "Cassie," he said.

"Yes, Uncle Charlie."

"Be careful."

"You be careful too." I was beginning to appreciate that warning. It seemed like every time we turned a corner, there was a new monster.

We hung up, and Frank looked at his watch. "It'll be at least two hours before they get here." He reached into the back of the SUV and retrieved a roll of crime scene tape. "Help me secure the site."

I was glad he didn't ask if I'd be all right. I'm a deputy, and this is part of the job. "What did Easterly say when you talked to him?" I asked.

"He's on his way over now."

"Can we trust him?" I asked.

"We have to."

* * *

Easterly arrived on the scene, along with the medical examiner, Dr. Zigler. The sheriff introduced us all.

"Cassie's uncle is on his way over," Frank explained. "He asked us to request an autopsy."

"Since it's an apparent suicide, there'll be an automatic autopsy," Dr. Zigler said. "Let's take a look." He handed masks and nitrile gloves to Frank and Sheriff Easterly, and the three of them walked to the barn while Pastor John and I stayed by the car.

The minister had regained his composure, but his face sagged.

"I'm sorry," I said. "I know this must be hard on you."

"I don't understand it, Cassie," he said. "I've seen men try to change the direction of their lives before. Many of them fail." He put his hand on the fender of the car as if to steady himself. "But I've never seen a transformation like Sinclair had. It was as if his eyes had been opened." He shook his head. "This is hard to accept."

The three men returned from the barn and pulled off their masks and gloves. Frank said, "Cassie's uncle knew Sinclair, and he doesn't believe this man would kill himself."

Easterly shook his head. "I appreciate that. People don't like to think their friends would do such a thing, but you saw the scene, Frank. The man is hanging, and the ladder he was standing on is kicked over to the side. There's no sign of a struggle. What possible evidence do you have that there could have been foul play? Besides, who would want to kill this man?" He spread his arm out around the yard. "He was driving an old Chevrolet pickup truck, for crying out loud. And he sure didn't look like a guy with a lot of money in his pocket."

"I know what you mean, but Charles Deakin is a responsible man. He knew Sinclair better than any of us, and he says the man wouldn't commit suicide." Frank looked back toward the barn. "Besides, he says Sinclair couldn't tie his shoelaces, and he sure wouldn't be able to make a noose."

Easterly wasn't buying it. He turned to the ME. "What d'ya think, Zig? Suicide, right?"

"Maybe," Dr. Zigler drawled out. He wiped his hands on his handkerchief and stuck it back in his pocket. "I'll need to examine the body before I make a ruling."

"When can we get your opinion?" Frank asked.

"I can probably have something by tomorrow afternoon. Let's say three o'clock."

"Even if we think Sinclair was murdered, wouldn't it be best if the medical examiner puts out word that it was an apparent suicide?" I asked. "That way nobody is tipped off that we may be looking for a murderer."

Zigler looked at the sheriff and raised his eyebrows as if asking for permission. Easterly crossed his arms over his chest. "She's got a point. If we think it could be murder, let's keep it quiet." He looked at me with a frown. "But remember, missy, you might be wrong. I still think this is a suicide."

I didn't like the "missy" part of that, but I was beginning to appreciate Easterly. He was new around here, but he was completely engaged.

Frank and the medical examiner nodded their approval.

Dr. Z's crew arrived in an ambulance and took the body down. Sheriff Easterly retrieved the wallet from Sinclair's pants pocket and showed us the cash and credit cards. Whatever happened here, theft was not a motive, and that supported Easterly's theory that this was suicide.

Zigler's team placed Sinclair's body in the ambulance and they left. Sheriff Easterly, Frank, and I scoured the area, looking for anything that might help us understand what went on there.

We didn't find Sinclair's cell phone. While Easterly searched the house, Frank and I went through Sinclair's truck. I found a small Bible in the glove compartment. It was the kind that has a zipper around it. We also found an empty bottle of Jim Beam bourbon on the ground by the truck.

We stored everything we found into evidence bags and gave them to Sheriff Easterly.

I pulled off the nitrile gloves and walked back to the Explorer. Pastor John was waiting for me. I told him about the empty bottle of liquor we'd found. He just shook his head.

My phone dinged. Uncle Charlie, Greg, and Dolly were outside of Shoalton and needed directions. I told him about the turnoff next to the large oak stump and asked about his arm.

His voice was strong. "I'm fine, Cassie. I just want to see what's going on there."

Within fifteen minutes, Greg pulled Dolly's Honda CR-V into the wide stretch of grass and dirt behind Easterly's squad car, and Uncle Charlie climbed out of the passenger seat. He was moving slow.

When I reached him, he put his good arm around me. "You okay?" I asked.

"Yes, I'm fine."

Uncle Charlie shook hands with Pastor John. "Where's Sinclair?"

"They took the body to the medical examiner's," I said. "He's going to perform the autopsy."

Uncle shook his head slowly. "I'd like to see where it happened."

We walked to the door of the barn and peered at the crime scene. Uncle was quiet, taking it all in. "Frank," he said, "can you take the rope down so I can get a closer look at it?"

"It's Sheriff Easterly's call," Frank said. "He's in charge."

Easterly nodded. "All right, Mr. Deakin. We'll get it down and bring it out by the car so you can look at it."

Chapter 34

The Noose

When they came out of the barn, Sheriff Easterly was holding the noose in his gloved hands. Frank spread a large sheet of plastic over the hood of the Explorer, and Easterly laid the noose there.

Frank handed me his phone that showed pictures of the noose hanging over a crossbeam in the barn.

Uncle Charlie looked over my shoulder. "See that knot?" He pointed to the way the rope was tied to the crossbeam. I nodded. "That's a hangman's knot. It's the kind that won't slip. The more pressure you put on it, the tighter it gets."

We had all gathered around Uncle as he explained. "Like I told Frank, Sinclair couldn't tie a knot in a pig's tail. He just didn't get how to do it. Even while he was at my farm, he had trouble when I asked him to tie Blondie to a post so I could sweep her stall. I ended up having to do it myself."

Easterly cut in. "You don't suppose he was just putting you on?"

"Nah. Sinclair was a proud man. He wasn't happy that guys in our squadron used to tease him about it. They called him Knotless." He pointed to the noose lying on the hood of the Explorer. "There's no way Sinclair tied that knot."

"Huh." Easterly rubbed his chin.

"Besides," Uncle Charlie continued, "look at the way the noose is wrapped," he said. "Sinclair was right-handed. Ten to one, this noose was tied by a left-handed man."

"How can you tell?" Frank asked.

Uncle picked up a stick that was lying on the ground. "Cut off about three feet of that crime scene tape, Frank, if you don't mind," he said.

Frank measured and cut the tape.

"Now wrap the tape around this stick."

Frank anchored the tape to the stick with his left hand. Then he wrapped the tape around it with his right hand in a counter-clockwise motion.

"You circled the stick counterclockwise," Uncle Charlie said. "Why?"

Frank shrugged. "Just seems natural to do it that way."

Uncle nodded. "That's true for a right-handed person like yourself. But a left-handed person would feel it was natural to wrap it the other way."

Easterly picked the noose up. "Clockwise."

The sun had begun to set, and Frank suggested we return to the Shoalton Cafe to have dinner and talk through possible scenarios of what we'd found. When we got there, we found a corner table away from the other patrons. We ordered, and while we waited for our food, we talked over the case.

Sheriff Easterly held onto the opinion that it was a probable suicide. "The simplest explanation is usually the right one," he said.

"What do we know about Sinclair's mental state?" Frank asked.

"Angry and depressed," I said, "because he couldn't get any of the authorities to agree to reopen the investigation into Lacey's death."

"That would certainly be a factor," Pastor John added. "Especially if you add alcohol into the equation."

"It wouldn't be the first time alcohol drove a person who was depressed to suicide," Easterly said.

"Sinclair wouldn't kill himself," Uncle Charlie said flatly. It was about the fiftieth time he'd said that since he got to the place, and I wanted to agree with him, but it made my head hurt to try to come up with a rational reason why anybody would murder Sinclair.

"Would a group of bikers murder someone just because they thought they could steal something valuable?" I asked.

"What bikers?" Easterly asked.

We explained what Sheriff Jessop had told us about Sinclair spending the night at a camp with bikers whom he shared his information with. Uncle Charlie just shook his head in disbelief. "What a stupid thing to do," he said. "You think those bikers attacked him?"

"I don't see how," Frank said. "We found Sinclair's wallet with money still in it, so it looks like theft is out. Besides, there's no sign of a struggle." He put his hand on my uncle's shoulder. "From what you've told me about Sinclair, he wouldn't let somebody just string him up without a fight."

"I understand all that," Uncle said, "and I can't explain it, but I do not believe Sinclair killed himself. There has to be another explanation."

Our spirits had sunk so low, we agreed to drop the speculation until we met with the medical examiner. We were all tired and didn't want to drive back to Uncle Charlie's farm. Sheriff Easterly suggested the Super 8 motel in Shoalton. "Nothing fancy, but it's a clean place, and it's quiet," he said. Then he left to go home.

While Greg was paying the bill, Frank walked outside to call Ruddy Buchanan and give him an update. Uncle Charlie and I stood in front of the display case while the woman behind the counter told us about how all the pies were baked by a local woman, Lois McCochran. "She makes the best peach pie in the universe," she said, and I saw Uncle Charlie flinch when he heard those words and looked at the four-pointed star in the pie crust. I wondered if he recognized the pattern. Whether he did or not, he'd be too much of a gentleman to say anything.

Greg, Dolly, Uncle Charlie, and Pastor John left in Dolly's CR-V to drive to the Super Eight Motel. Frank and I rode alone in the Explorer.

"What did Ruddy say?" I asked.

Frank drove with one hand on the wheel. "He said he got a report back from the people he had sent to talk to the parole board. As far as they could find out, the two bikers who attacked Charlie weren't known to be friends in prison. Ruddy wants to know how they got together after they were released."

"Maybe they joined a gang of bikers and met each other there," I said.

Frank nodded slowly. "Possibly. Ruddy wants us to find the campground where Sinclair met the bikers, so I called Ralph. He said none of the guys who come to his place recognized the pictures of those two. I told him about Sinclair talking to a group of bikers at a campground. He said Archie and Buck know the lay of the land out here. He's going to ride over tomorrow with them to take a look."

"We can trust them, can't we?" I asked.

Frank didn't answer.

When we arrived at the Super 8 parking lot, I could see it wasn't tourist season in Shoalton. The others met us in the lobby.

They had already made the room arrangements. Frank and Uncle Charlie stayed in one room, Greg and Pastor John in another, and Dolly and I stayed in the third.

I fell asleep trying to put a puzzle together where none of the pieces fit.

Chapter 35

Following Sinclair

The next morning, Frank asked Greg and Dolly to go to the Shoalton Cafe and pick up breakfast rolls and coffee so that the rest of us wouldn't have to answer any questions from Jake about whether or not we found Sinclair. We all gathered in one room to scarf down the goodies when they returned.

We were all on edge. Even Uncle Charlie had receded into himself. Unusual for him.

Sheriff Easterly called to tell us how to get to Dr. Zigler's office at three o'clock that afternoon.

Ralph, Buck, and Archie arrived on their motorcycles at about nine o'clock. We huddled in the parking lot with a map of the area. According to Sheriff Jessop, Sinclair had spent the night at a campsite after he left Sheriff Easterly's office. Buck and Archie pointed out a couple of places they knew where bikers could camp.

I wanted Uncle Charlie to stay at the motel with Greg and Dolly, but he was adamant that he wanted to come along.

Frank drove the Explorer, and I rode shotgun. Uncle Charlie and Pastor John were in the back seat. Greg and Dolly followed us in Dolly's CR-V. We were a grim bunch, but at least we were doing something.

Sheriff Easterly said Sinclair came to his office on Tuesday, so it must have been about a week earlier when he had stayed at a campsite. Since it hadn't rained since then, there might be some motorcycle tracks we could identify.

The first campground was just a small dirt patch by the side of the road. There was some trash lying around, but it didn't look like it had seen humanity for a long time. We drove on.

When we got to the next campsite, we found some motorcycle tracks and boot prints, but nothing else.

"I don't think anybody stayed over here," Archie said. "Bikers aren't the cleanest folks around, and there's no trash at all. No sign of life."

We all nodded in agreement. Ralph looked at the tracks and declared one of them could be the same as the one he saw at Uncle Charlie's farm, but there were lots of bikes like that. Impossible to tell.

We examined the boot marks. Most of them were smudged, but one was very clear, so I made an outline of it. Even though I thought it wouldn't amount to anythng, it seemed like it might make Uncle Charlie feel better.

Frank asked if Archie and Buck knew of any other camp-grounds.

"There's only one more area I know about," Archie said. "It's just outside of Prescott."

The last one was a little farther south and a mile off the high-way. We had to follow the bikers onto a dirt road to get to it. It ended in a wide opening that looked more promising. There was a large trash container that had some whiskey bottles lying on top of papers and candy wrappers.

"You guys ever stop here?" Frank asked Archie and Buck.

"I've been here once or twice," Buck said.

"But how would Sinclair know this place was here?" I asked. "We would never have found it if we hadn't been following you guys."

"Yeah. I don't get that either," Frank said. "Maybe he met them somewhere else, and they led him here."

We all chewed on that idea for a while. We didn't see any clear motorcycle tracks, but the ground was so dry and dusty, the wind could have blown through and erased any tracks.

Frank asked Greg to bag some of the empty bottles to see if they could get fingerprints. If we could tie those bottles to the two guys who attacked Uncle Charlie, we'd be making progress.

"Any other places you can think of?" Frank asked.

Archie and Buck shook their heads in unison. "We'll ride the area today," Archie said, "and let you know if we come up with anything."

As we drove away, something bothered me about that last place. The empty bottles of alcohol. "Frank," I said as we were driving along after the bikers.

"Yeah?"

"If Sinclair spent the night at a campsite with a bunch of bikers who said they were Christians, would they be doing a lot of drinking?"

Frank bit on his bottom lip. "Good point. Maybe the Christian bikers were for real, but there were others there who overheard the conversation."

"That's the best explanation I've heard yet," I said, and I worked it out in my head. There was a campground with a group of bikers who were believers, and Sinclair talked to them about the "valuable" thing he had left at Uncle Charlie's. But the conversation was overheard by some others who weren't inclined to do the right thing.

Frank had told me that a lot of detective work is finding little details that tell the story. But it can be dull and tedious to keep searching. Still, we'd come up with a plausible scenario, and we had retrieved some bottles that might provide fingerprints. That was something.

Uncle Charlie said he wanted to make arrangements with the local funeral home for Sinclair's burial, so we got in touch with them and spent the rest of our time picking out a casket and working with the funeral director.

Finally, three o'clock arrived.

* * *

Sheriff Easterly was just getting out of his squad car when we pulled into the parking lot of the morgue. "Find anything?" he asked.

Frank gave him a quick rundown of our tour through campsites and the possibility of evidence from some of the liquor bottles we found.

Dr. Z met us in the outer office of the morgue. He had on medical scrubs and was wiping his hands on a paper towel. We introduced him to Uncle Charlie, Greg, and Dolly.

"What did the autopsy reveal?" Easterly asked.

Dr. Z tossed the paper towel into a wastebasket. "Sinclair Alderson died approximately one week ago. You told me he had met with Sheriff Jessop last Wednesday, and I believe he died shortly after that. Maybe Wednesday afternoon or Thursday." He paused to take a breath. "It appears the cause of death was asphyxiation, and there were ligature marks on his neck. That would be consistent with dying by hanging and would support the suicide verdict."

Uncle Charlie shook his head. "I don't believe it."

Zigler slowly removed his glasses and looked at Uncle Charlie. "As it turns out, Mr. Deakin, neither do I."

The room went completely silent. "I thought you said it was consistent with suicide," Easterly said.

"That's correct. And since there was no sign of a struggle, it would be reasonable to assume that Sinclair Alderson took his own life." He looked at Uncle Charlie. "If you hadn't insisted that Sinclair wouldn't have killed himself and they told me about the rope, I probably would have ruled it a suicide."

"But you found something else?" Frank asked.

"Yes. I did a quick blood analysis. Although I'll have to get the final result from the state lab, I found a very high dose of barbiturates and toxic substance in Sinclair's blood stream. Enough to kill a good-sized horse."

"Could he have done that to himself?" I asked. "Maybe he was using drugs in addition to the alcohol."

"I found a puncture wound in his neck. About the size a hypodermic needle would make."

"So, someone jabbed him with poison?" Easterly was shaking his head. "But wouldn't Sinclair have fought that? Wouldn't we see signs of a struggle?"

"Not necessarily. My theory is that someone came to see him. Possibly someone he knew. Maybe somebody had already given him a spiked drink. When he turned his back, that person stuck him with a hypodermic so loaded with poison that Sinclair simply crumpled to the ground immediately."

"Then why hang him? Why not just leave?"

"Again, it's just my theory, but I'm guessing someone very much wanted this to look like suicide. After Sinclair was unconscious, the killer tied the rope around his neck and hung him. That way an autopsy would reveal he died of asphyxiation, and the ligature marks on his neck would make it look like he hung himself."

Dr. Z fell silent, and I tried to take this all in. "If what you say is true," I said, "then we're looking for a left-handed killer. Someone who possibly knew Sinclair."

"And we're looking for someone who's very clever," Frank said. "I'm not sure how many people would have taken the time to make sure the ligature marks were obvious on Sinclair's neck."

"And somebody who had access to medicine," Easterly replied.

Dr. Z lowered himself into one of the chairs and pulled off the surgical cap. "That's true. But just about anybody in these parts who has horses would have access to substances that would be powerful enough to knock out a human being."

There was a moment's silence as we all chewed on this new information.

"Wouldn't it have been hard for somebody to haul Sinclair up by the rope and hang him?" I asked.

"It would have taken some serious strength. That's for sure," Zigler said.

"Could it have been more than one person?" Frank asked.

"Yes."

"But we didn't find any footprints or fingerprints," Easterly added.

"Somebody was very careful." Dr. Z ran his hand over the back of his neck. "They knew what they were doing."

"Do we still try to keep this thing a secret?" I asked.

"No." Easterly began to pace the floor. "We might get more information if we get the word out that it's a suspected murder. Maybe the killer will get nervous and make a move."

"I agree," Frank said.

"Frank, I'm going to call Ruddy Buchanan and ask if he'll let you work with me on this case. That all right with you?"

"Count me in," Frank said. He looked at me and I nodded. "And my assistant deputy too."

Chapter 36

The Funeral

Our little team had driven back to Uncle Charlie's farm after talking to Dr. Zigler. Frank spent time with the warden of the state penitentiary to get a better understanding of the two men who attacked Uncle Charlie. Greg had the forensics team examine the fingerprints on the empty liquor bottles, but they hadn't turned up anything of value. Three days later, we were back in Balmoral County, standing in a semicircle around an open gravesite in the Eternal Peace Cemetery.

It was a small group. Sinclair didn't have any family, and the only friends seemed to be Uncle Charlie and Pastor John. No one knew of any acquaintance in Alaska to contact. Sheriff Easterly had contacted Lois and Halcyon, the McCochran sisters, since they had known Sinclair. Sheriff Mannie Jessop and Sheriff Easterly both attended. Mannie told us his son, Bob, wanted to come, but he was bogged down with office work and couldn't make it. Besides, he hadn't really been involved in the whole Sinclair saga.

Pastor John held the Bible in steady hands. He was wearing a tie and jacket, but he said he didn't own any dress slacks, so he was in blue jeans. The rest of us stood quietly and watched as the casket was lowered into the ground.

Uncle Charlie and I stood together. Frank was on my other side. Greg and Dolly stood on the opposite side next to the McCochran sisters. Sheriff Easterly and the older Sheriff Jessop were standing with them.

Pastor John read from the book of John. "Let not your hearts be troubled. Believe in God; believe also in me. In my Father's house are many rooms. If it were not so, would I have told you that I go to prepare a place for you? And if I go and prepare a place for you, I will come again and will take you to myself, that where I am you may be also."

I thought about those rooms in heaven and wondered if Lacey and Sinclair would meet again.

Pastor John stepped to the side and asked Uncle Charlie to say a few words.

Uncle Charlie walked to his place at the head of the gravesite and cleared his throat. He had looked ragged and old in the three days since we found Sinclair's body. Today he wore a suit and tie, and he was freshly shaved. The word that came to my mind was "constant."

"How do you say goodbye to the man who saved your life?" he began. "Sinclair Alderson was a man who fought his way through his time on this earth, from his father's abusive behavior to a war that stole whatever innocence he had left. And when he got home from that horror, he found he had lost his little sister." Uncle paused and swallowed hard.

"When Sinclair moved to Alaska, I was afraid he was lost forever, and he almost was. But several weeks ago, Sinclair found something. Something precious. The greatest gift a person can receive." He looked at Pastor John. "Sinclair found what he didn't even know he was looking for. He found God, and he found salvation."

Uncle's face wrinkled in a frown. "I saw Sinclair kill men in Vietnam. I heard him rage when he found out his little sister had died. I saw him turn his back on everything and move as far away as he could to block out the memory of his life. But that's not the way I'll remember him now.

"When Sinclair left my farm to look for the truth behind Lacey's death, he was at peace with himself. He was a new man, and it's the way I'll always remember him." Uncle bent to the ground and picked up a fistful of dirt. "I can't save your life, my friend, but I promise you we will do everything we can to find the truth." He dropped the dirt on the casket. Then he put his Stetson on and walked slowly back toward the car.

Chapter 37

The McCochran Sisters

Halcyon and Lois McCochran invited us to their home after the funeral to have coffee and cake. Mannie Jessop said he had to take his wife to visit her sick brother, but he offered to help in any way he could to get to the bottom of Sinclair's death. The rest of us formed a caravan behind the sisters' old Toyota Corolla to their farmhouse.

The house smelled of fresh bread and cut flowers. Lois must have been up early baking for the Shoalton Cafe.

Large windows surrounded the living room, and the bright sunlight lifted our spirits. An old Victorian-style couch overlaid with crocheted afghans sat in front of the fireplace, and various chairs were placed around the room.

Dolly had made a fabulous coffee cake, and she and Lois latched on to each other right away and began talking ingredients. Must be some sort of species identification that I missed out on.

Halcyon stood in the middle of the living room, directing traffic. She looked about as different from Lois as was possible. No one would have pegged them as sisters. While Lois was tall, thin as a stick, and wore dark polyester slacks, Halcyon was short and pudgy, with frills around the collar and cuffs of her dress. Lois wore her hair pulled back in a tight bun, but Halcyon's hair was dyed a soft blonde and cut short and curled around her face.

Halcyon took me aside. "It was mighty decent of you and your uncle to arrange for the funeral. I expect that might have been about the nicest thing anybody ever did for Sinclair."

"Tell me about Sinclair," I asked, as Halcyon led me toward the kitchen.

She pulled a can of coffee from the pantry shelf and ladled coffee grounds into a large percolator while she talked.

"Sinclair had a hard life here," she said. "His father wasn't much of a farmer, and he somehow got about the least productive little patch of dry scrabble you could find in these parts. I swear, I don't know how he got hold of that land, but you couldn't hardly grow a stalk of wheat in that dust." She looked around. "Hand me that tray, would you, honey?"

She continued to chatter as I helped her load cups on the tray. In another time and place, Halcyon would have made a good dormitory house mother. Or maybe an even better general in the army. She had a way of simply drawing you into her to-do list until you were searching the kitchen for cups, saucers, and spoons.

"I think we'd all like to hear about Sinclair's family," I said.

"Let's get some of this food to these hungry folks, and we'll talk."

The others were all gathered in the living room. Frank and Sheriff Easterly were examining the books on the shelf next to the fireplace. Dolly and Greg were looking at family pictures on the wall. Uncle Charlie and Pastor John were sitting next to each other on the couch, looking through a farm magazine.

When everyone had settled in and began to enjoy the goodies, Uncle Charlie said, "I sure would like it if you'd tell us a little about Sinclair's family. You're the only people around here who knew them."

Halcyon claimed a big rocking chair that had her form imprinted on it.

"I gather the Aldersons were pretty poor," I said.

She stopped rocking and looked at me. "Honey, there wasn't nothin' pretty about it."

"Tell us what it was like," Uncle said

Halcyon leaned back and started to rock again. "Malcolm Alderson—that was Sinclair's father—seemed a decent fellow at first. I guess he and his wife moved here when Sinclair was around fourteen or fifteen years old. I'm thinking Malcolm was looking for a place to start over." She looked at me and put her hand on my arm. "We don't pry into other folks' pasts, you know."

Lois made a coughing sound and sipped her coffee. "It wasn't a good decision on Malcolm's part. He didn't know anything about farming, and he sure didn't pick up much around here."

Halcyon continued the thread. "It was like the land was fightin' him, and we felt bad for them. Sinclair got odd jobs to help the family, but the little girl. Well, she was pretty much left on her own."

"What was Sinclair's mother like?" I asked.

"She was a little slow, if you know what I mean. And she had some health problems. I think that may have been part of the problem. Malcolm had this useless strip of dirt to farm and a sickly wife to take care of." She grimaced. "Then he got to drinking. And pretty soon there were rumors about him being drunk and cantankerous. We think maybe he couldn't handle the shame of his own failure."

"People said he took it out on Sinclair," Lois said and clicked her tongue. "I expect the boy couldn't take it anymore and that's why he joined the army."

"That's what he told me," Pastor John said.

"And then there was Lacey," Lois said.

"Sinclair's sister." Uncle Charlie leaned forward in his chair.

Halcyon nodded. "She was the sweetest little thing you ever saw, but she didn't get much supervision. Malcolm used to bring her over here to stay because we enjoyed her company and her mother was always sick."

"So you got to know Lacey well?"

"Oh, yes," Lois said. "She stayed with us sometimes in the summer when she wasn't in school." She paused. "You know Lacey had a learning problem."

"Sinclair told me about that," Uncle Charlie said.

"We didn't know the right words, but we knew she had some issues. She was a very smart little girl, though. She even learned to read." Lois laughed and touched Halcyon's arm. "Remember how she used to get the letters mixed up?"

Halcyon's eyes twinkled. "Oh, it was funny. Lacey saw our name McCochran on the mailbox, and she called us the 'Macaroni sisters.'" She laughed so hard, her eyes teared up, and she took a lace handkerchief out of her pocket and wiped at them. When she had regained her composure, she took a deep breath. "The child touched our hearts. When we learned about her accident, it just about tore us up."

Lois took a tissue out from under her sleeve and blew her nose. "We were terribly upset the day she died. You see, she was here with us that morning."

Chapter 38

Lacey Was Here

The air seemed to whoosh out of the room. Lois's declaration that Lacey had been with them the day she died crashed into me. I think most of us had only been half listening, thinking things through on our own. Now everyone's head snapped up at attention.

I looked at Sheriff Easterly. His chin was down around his belt, and his eyes bulged. "Lacey was here with you the day she died?" he asked.

"Yes," Halcyon said. "You can imagine how we felt when we found out she had fallen over the side of that cliff."

Lois shifted in her chair. "I'm surprised nobody mentioned that to you. But then it's been such a long time ago."

"Can you tell us about that day?" Frank asked.

Lois nodded to her sister. "You tell it, Halcyon. You were closer to the child than I was."

Halcyon sat up straighter in the rocking chair. "It was a long time ago, but I still remember it like yesterday. Lacey came over that morning. We were in the kitchen. Lois was making bread, and

I was cleaning up after her when we heard the knock. Lois was up to her ears in dough, so I let Lacey in."

"I remember," Lois said. "Lacey was so excited, she ran into the kitchen all breathless."

Halcyon rocked back and forth. Her short legs came up off the floor each time she went back. "Lacey could get excited about things, but she was especially happy that day. She ran into the kitchen and didn't even take a cookie. Now that was unusual. Do you remember what she was talking about that day, Lois?"

"Yes. It was one of her favorite topics. The prince and the princess."

When Lois dropped that out there, the room suddenly came into sharp HD focus, and everything moved in slow motion. Greg's hand stopped halfway to his mouth, and he put the brownie he was holding back on his napkin.

Lois looked around, realizing the atmosphere had shifted. "What? Did I say something wrong?"

Frank swallowed hard. "Do you remember what she said about the prince and princess?"

Halcyon started rocking again. She tilted her head slightly. "Oh, it was one of her favorite topics. Lacey used to love for us to read stories to her, and she especially liked to hear about the prince and the princess." She looked around the room. "I think we have that old book of fairy tales here somewhere. It had just about everything. Cinderella, Rapunzel."

Lois smiled. "Lacey liked stories. We'd read to her out of the fairy tale book or the Bible. We figured she wasn't getting much religious training at home, you know." She clicked her tongue. "Even though her attention span usually wasn't long, she would sit very still and listen when we read to her."

Halcyon nodded. "We bought a little Bible for her birthday one year, and she loved that little Bible. It had a zipper around it so you could close it up completely. She thought that made it special."

Frank and I looked at each other. The Bible we found in Sinclair's car.

Lois pushed a plate of cookies over toward me. "Lacey liked the story about Noah's Ark. She said she was going to build an ark herself so she could go visit Sinclair."

"She loved her brother. She missed him in her own way." Halcyon sighed. "I think she was a very bright child. A special child."

Lois frowned. "The poor thing was left too much on her own. Her parents would let her wander all over the place at all hours of the day and night." She shook her head and made that clicking noise with her tongue again.

Halcyon stopped rocking. The two women were talking to each other now, as if the rest of us weren't there. "She'd go into those woods and gather things."

Lois clapped her hands together. "Yes! I haven't thought about that for years. Remember how she used to bring us things? Pine cones or pretty rocks. She said they were special gifts just for us, and we kept them on the mantel so she could see them. Look. Some of them are still there."

All the heads in the room turned to look at a few rocks that sat on one end of the mantel, just beside two candlesticks.

Both sisters grew silent then. I thought I could feel Lacey's presence in the room, and I imagined her emptying her pockets of the treasure she'd collected and begging for a story.

Halcyon tilted her head down, and she seemed to age right there in her rocking chair. "Such a shame."

We all felt the weight of that sorrow. In my mind, I could see the two spinsters sitting on the couch with the child between them, reading stories that took Lacey out of her limited reality to another world.

"I think Lacey was closer to God than most of us will ever be," Pastor John said quietly.

"Yes. I'm quite sure she was." Lois sat back in her straight chair and crossed her ankles.

Frank cleared his throat. He had sat quietly through the reminiscence, but I knew he was laser-focused on the day Lacey died. "Can you tell us more about the prince and princess Lacey talked about that day?"

Halcyon began rocking again, trying to regain the memory. "I guess she was remembering one of the fairy tales. I don't know which one. Lacey told us she saw a prince bring a princess into the woods, or something like that. We didn't think much about it at the time, but she was probably thinking about that little patch of scraggly trees over there behind the Alderson farm where she spent so much time." She straightened her skirt. "She wanted us to write the story for her."

"Did you write it?" Frank asked.

"Oh yes. We found a little slip of paper somewhere and wrote it down. It was just a sentence or two, but she was determined that it was her story."

Uncle Charlie pulled the paper out of his pocket. "Does this look like what you wrote?"

Lois took the paper, looked at it and then stared at Uncle Charlie. Her mouth made a perfect O. I heard the strong intake of breath. "Where did you get this?"

Chapter 39

Lacey's Story

For the second time that afternoon, I felt a shock wave go through the room that rendered us all mute. Halcyon took the paper from Lois and opened her mouth to say something, but no words came out. We were all dumb in the presence of something that we didn't understand. I felt Lacey close by. Maybe right beside me in the fading light, and I was almost afraid to move because I didn't want her to leave. Frank reached over and placed a hand on my arm. I was trembling.

Uncle Charlie's face reddened as he took the paper back from Halcyon. Halcyon repeated Lois's question. "Where did you get that?"

Uncle Charlie told her how Sinclair had found the note and believed it might have something to do with Lacey's death. He told them how Sinclair had left the note with him.

"This could be a clue to Lacey's death," Frank said.

Halcyon's eyebrows knitted together in confusion. "How could that be? It was just a little story. Nothing important."

"It may be very important, Ms. McCochran." Sheriff Easterly had been so quiet, I almost forgot he was in the room. He stooped down in front of Halcyon and put his hand on the arms of the rocking chair. "This could give us insight into what happened the day Lacey died." His voice was so low, I almost couldn't make it out. "Please tell us everything you remember that Lacey said about the prince and princess."

Halcyon pursed her lips together. "Goodness. It was so long ago." She looked over at Lois. "Lois has a better memory than I do. Lois, do you remember that day?"

"Of course. Lacey was wearing that brown dress you made for her, and those red shoes."

"Lois bought her those shoes," Halcyon said. "We have a picture of her around here somewhere wearing that dress and those shoes."

Lois looked at Pastor John. "I've thought about that day a million times. Sometimes I think it was our fault that Lacey died that day. Maybe if she had stayed longer and we had read more stories to her, it wouldn't have happened. But we were delivering some baked goods that day, so we dropped Lacey off at her parents' place and went about our business."

He patted her hand. "You were her good friends. You shouldn't feel guilty."

I felt Frank shift his weight forward beside me. I knew he was trying to sound calm, but his voice had a tension in it. "We'd like to know anything you can remember about the prince and princess."

"Can I see the paper again?" Lois asked, and Uncle Charlie handed it to her. She read out loud, "The prince brought the princess in the wild wood." She looked up. "We didn't think much about it. To Lacey, that one sentence was an entire book." She handed the note to her sister. "Halcyon wrote it," she said. "Her handwriting is better than mine."

"Lois is left-handed. Her handwriting is atrocious, so I always write everything that needs writing."

"And the date at the top of the page?" Frank asked. "August 12, 1970."

"Lacey didn't ask for that," Halcyon said, "but I told her I'd write it there so she'd always know the date of her first story." Her voice trailed off. "That was the day she died."

"And the cross at the bottom?" Frank asked.

"I don't remember that. Do you, sister?"

"No," Lois answered. "Lacey must have added that later."

"Thank you very much, ladies," Sheriff Easterly said. He stood and hooked his thumbs in the waistband of his slacks. "You've been very helpful."

"You don't think this little slip of paper had anything to do with Lacey's death do you? I couldn't bear it if it did." Halcyon's voice shook.

"No," Easterly said. "Not at all."

The sun was low on the horizon, and the western sky was the color of ripe mango when we left the McCochran sisters waving to us from their front porch. Uncle Charlie, Dolly, Pastor John, and Greg headed back to the farm in Dolly's CR-V while Frank, Sheriff Easterly, and I huddled next to the Explorer.

I looked at Frank. "Are you thinking what I'm thinking?"

He nodded. "Lacey saw something in those woods."

"That's right," Easterly said. "Now all we have to do is figure out what she saw."

Chapter 40

August 12, 1970

L acey said goodbye to her friends and ran into her parents' house. The Macaroni sisters had written her story, and she found a pencil and carefully drew a star on it. Then she put the story in the Bible right next to the handkerchief.

Now that Sinclair was gone, she got to have her own room. The cardboard box in the corner had all her special things. There were the rocks she had chosen and some special leaves. She zipped up the Bible and carefully placed it in the box. Then she ran out of the house.

The day was turning warm, and Lacey practiced her skipping into the woods. She was sure the prince would return to wake up the princess. A real-live prince and princess.

She ran to her favorite spot behind the biggest pine tree and looked around. This was where she saw him last night. He had dropped his handkerchief when he took the princess out of the truck and carried her into the woods on the other side of the path.

She put her hand over her mouth to stop the giggles and hoped the prince wouldn't be angry that she had picked up his handkerchief. Maybe it was magic.

She didn't want to wake the princess, so she tiptoed across the path and peeked through the trees. But she didn't see the princess. He must have put her somewhere special.

Maybe he was waiting until nighttime to wake her up. Lacey walked back to the path and retraced her steps toward her house when she heard the sound of a vehicle. She stood still in the middle of the road while it pulled to a stop in front of her. The prince got out and walked toward her.

"Are you going to wake the princess up?" Lacey asked. "I saw you put her to sleep last night. Are you going to kiss her now?" Lacey clapped her hands.

"You saw me?" the prince asked.

"Yes. I saw you carry her over there." Lacey pointed to the thicket where the prince had taken the princess. "Are you going to kiss her and wake her up? Can I watch?" Lacey blushed and put her finger in her mouth.

The prince stood looking at her for a long time until she wondered if she had said something wrong. She didn't want to get in trouble.

"Would you like to come with me to see the princess?" he said.

"Oh, yes!" Lacey clapped her hands and jumped up and down. "Can I?"

"Yes," he said. "She's just right down at the end of the lane. Come along and I'll show you." He held out his hand.

She took it. It was large and warm, and he held her hand firmly in his. They walked together to the end of the path.

When they got close to the cliff, Lacey hung back. "Danger," she said.

"Don't worry," the prince said. "I'll protect you. We just have to go a little farther to see the princess." Then he led her to the edge of the cliff.

Chapter 41

The Prince and the Princess

I t was twilight when we arrived at the Alderson farm. That strange interval between day and night when you want the sun to stay with you, but the calm of the evening makes you long to be home.

Sheriff Easterly, Frank, and I found the path leading into the woods. It was so overgrown that it was almost indistinguishable from the surroundings.

We parked the cars. Frank and Easterly both had flashlights, so we made our way toward the cliff, our shoes crackling the dead leaves and underbrush beneath our feet. The smell of pine and rotting wood filled my head.

As we moved down the path, I had that same feeling like Lacey was right there with us, walking beside me toward the steep drop to the river. At one point, the sensation was so strong, I turned and looked behind me.

"What is it?" Frank asked.

"Nothing. I just thought I heard something."

We continued on toward the cliff. Frank stopped a few feet

from the edge and leaned back against a boulder. "Let's try to get the timeline. Cassie?"

"I think Lacey saw a man and woman come into the woods. Then she told the McCochran sisters about it."

"But they said she came to see them in the morning. Remember, Lois was making bread for the cafe."

"So maybe Lacey saw something the night before. They said she was out at all times of day and night," Easterly said.

"Okay," Frank said. "Lacey saw something the afternoon or evening before she died. The next morning she ran to tell the McCochran sisters about it. Why was she so excited?"

"I believe Lacey was excited because she thought she saw a real prince and princess," I said, "and she couldn't wait to tell the McCochran sisters."

"What I can't figure out is why she thought it was a real prince and princess," Frank said. "She must have seen people coming in these woods before. They said she was out here all the time. Why was this different?"

We all fell silent. I heard a rustling in the bushes on the side of the path. Was it the wind? Or were there still animals in this forsaken patch of nothingness? A chill ran down my back, and I moved closer to Frank.

Easterly looked at me. I could barely make out his features as dusk closed in. "I don't mean to be insensitive to your gender, Cassie, but you're a female, and there's something that fascinates young girls about the fairy tale princes and princesses. Can you think of anything that would get her all excited?"

"When I was a little girl, the librarian used to read fairy tales to us," I said. I tried to recall the feelings of excitement when the prince and princess finally got together and lived happily ever after. That's what would delight a child like Lacey.

As the light faded, a gentle breeze silently curled around us. The only thought that came to mind was how peaceful it was. I could almost hear my Sunday school teacher's voice when she talked about God's presence. "He makes me lie down in green pastures."

"Sleeping Beauty," I said so loud that it startled even me.

"What?" Frank said.

"The McCochran sisters said they used to read fairy tales to Lacey, right?"

"Yes." Easterly's voice sounded skeptical.

"In the story of Sleeping Beauty, the prince wakes the princess up with a kiss." I began to pace back and forth in front of them. I stopped and looked at Frank.

"What are you getting at?" he asked.

"Lacey saw a man and woman. Maybe the man carried the woman into the woods and laid her down."

"Laid her down?" Frank's voice dropped. "You mean ..."

"Yes." I saw the scene in front of me. "I'll bet anything that the McCochran sisters had read the story of Sleeping Beauty to Lacey not long before she died. Lacey was so focused on that story that she thought the man was a prince and was carrying a sleeping princess who he would come back later to wake up with a kiss." I felt my heart banging against my chest.

"Why would Lacey think she was asleep?" Easterly asked.

I bit my lower lip, trying to make out the scene, and then it came to me. "Imagine this. A man drives into the woods. Lacey sees him take a woman out of the vehicle. Since the man is carrying the woman, Lacey thinks it's the princess who's in a deep sleep. The man carries the woman away from the road and into the woods. Lacey thinks he's going to come back later to kiss the princess and wake her up."

"Go on," Frank said. His voice registered doubt. Did this make any sense?

"Later, the man does exactly what Lacey thought he would—he returns. Remember Uncle Charlie said there was a handkerchief. Maybe the man realized he had dropped his handkerchief and came back to find it. But when he learns a young girl had seen him, he kills her." I couldn't believe I was saying those words. Me, of all people, creating a fairy tale just so I could prove Sinclair was right.

But this wasn't about Sinclair anymore. This was about Lacey.

Easterly started to pace. "That's a pretty wild theory." He was shaking his head like he thought I had lost it. Then he stopped and looked directly at me. "But ever since Sinclair came to see me, I've kept going over and over what he said. He was so sure that Lacey had been murdered. And now we know somebody is trying awfully hard to stop us from understanding why Sinclair thought that."

Frank nodded. "You said a young woman had disappeared at the same time Lacey died." His voice had a now-we're-getting-somewhere quality to it.

"Right." Easterly nodded. "Her name was Jane Satterfield. Apparently, she had tried to run away previously, so everybody thought she had finally succeeded."

My Sunday school teacher used to tell us God's truth illuminates the darkness. Even though the sharp edge of night had dropped over us, it was all beginning to become light.

"I'll arrange to get some dogs," Easterly said. "Can you meet me here in the morning? Say ten o'clock?"

Chapter 42

Jane Satterfield

Frank and I stopped at the Super 8 motel. It would be exhausting to go all the way to Uncle's farm and then return to the Alderson place the next morning. We both had changes of clothes with us.

Frank took my hand as we walked to the front door. "I'm going to stay with you tonight, Cassie."

"What?" That was overboard, even for Frank.

"Look, I'm not trying to make a move on you, but we're getting close to solving this case. I can feel it. I don't want to take any chances."

I felt it too. Some awful thing was out there just waiting for us to uncover it. And there was something else. A force that would explode when we finally put the puzzle together. I hoped the explosion wouldn't destroy us.

"You're not planning to register us as Mr. and Mrs. White, I hope."

"I don't think you have to do that anymore." He grinned down at me. "Times have changed."

The attendant on duty checked us in and we found room 27 at the far end of the building. There was one king-size bed, a couch, and an assortment of chairs and end tables.

Thankfully, Frank was all business. He checked the closet and bathroom. Then he looked behind the drapes. "It's a solid plate glass window," he said and made sure the drapes were completely closed. "I'll sleep here." He pointed to the couch. "Help me move it."

I dropped my duffel bag on the floor and we shoved the sofa in front of the door.

Frank took a pillow off the bed and tossed it on the couch. He found a blanket in the closet and laid it next to the pillow. "There. That should do it." He sat on the sofa and bounced up and down. "Comfy."

Being alone in a motel room with a man was a completely new experience for me. Even on the rare occasions when my dad and I traveled, he either booked a suite so I could have the bedroom to myself or he got us adjoining rooms. He said it was a matter of propriety.

Although I didn't think Frank would try anything out of line, I still felt uncomfortable. It's rare for me to be at a loss for words, but this was one of those occasions. "I'm going to take a shower," I said and hoisted my duffle bag onto the bed.

Frank tried to lighten the mood. "Did you bring your frilly pink nightgown?"

"Very funny." I pulled out my striped pajamas and waved them at him.

I left him there and went into the bathroom. The idea that we had stood where a murder may have been committed made me feel dirty. I turned the water as hot as I could stand it and tried to scrub away the smell of rotten wood from that dry patch of trees and death.

I dried off, dressed, and eased the door open. Frank was sitting on the couch with his head leaning back against the door. His eyes were closed. When I pushed the door all the way open, it creaked and he sat up.

He held out his arm. "Come here, Cassie."

I hesitated.

"Don't worry. I'm not going to try anything."

I walked to the couch, and he patted the cushion next to him for me to sit. I eased down beside him and let him hold my hand.

There were dark circles under his eyes, and I wondered how much sleep he had been getting. I felt sure it was a lot less than me, and I'd felt sleep-deprived for days.

"I want to tell you something about me," he said.

Normally, I would have come back with a snarky reply, but the tone of his voice made me stop. "Okay."

"Cassie, I decided a long time ago that I couldn't enter into a serious relationship with a woman. The kind of work I do is dangerous, and I don't want to risk the life of someone I have feelings for." He stroked my hand. "It's important to me that you understand that."

"Is this about your parents?"

He stopped rubbing my hand. "How did you know?" He squinted his eyes. "Did Greg tell you?"

"I won't say who told me, but I found out that your parents were murdered." I put my hand on top of his. "I'm sorry. It must have been awful for you to lose your parents like that, and I've been a jerk."

"It had to be Greg," Frank said. "He shouldn't have said anything, but I guess it's just as well. I wanted to explain it to you, but I never found just the right moment."

"I guess I wasn't very helpful, huh?"

"No. It seemed like things never worked out for us."

"The day you saw Greg and me together behind the barn, we were talking about the story of your parents. I realized what a massive idiot I had been, and I hugged Greg." I grimaced. "That's when you appeared."

"You mean you and Greg aren't involved with each other?"

I shook my head in disbelief. Men can be so dumb. "I think you need a better attraction radar. Haven't you noticed the way Greg and Dolly are always together?"

He chuckled. "I guess I've had other things on my mind." He stroked my hand again.

"Do you mind if I ask you a question about your parents?"

"No, I don't mind." He reached up and gently pushed my hair back.

"Do you think your mother would have changed the course of her life if she'd known how it would end?"

Frank's eyes seemed to focus somewhere far away. "I don't know." He put his arm around me, pulled my head down onto his shoulder, and kissed my hair. Then his breath deepened, and he was asleep.

I woke up at 6:30 to the sound of a loud click. I sat up and stretched. After Frank had fallen asleep the night before, I had eased out from under his arm and had made my way silently to the bed.

The couch had been moved away from the door. "Frank?" I called out. I thought maybe he was in the shower, but there was no water running. "Frank?" I called louder.

The clothes he had been wearing the day before were neatly laid out on the sofa.

I blinked hard and peered out of the window. The Explorer

was still there, but no Frank. I got dressed and was combing my hair in the bathroom when I heard the door open.

"Breakfast, sleepyhead," Frank said, as he came in with coffee and donuts.

"My hero." I took one of the cups and sipped the caffeine.

"You look great." He reached out and tousled my hair. "I went to sleep last night with my face in your hair," he said. "It smelled like lemon icing."

I rolled my eyes. "Glad to know I can attract men with my dessert aroma."

We were at the Alderson farm at nine-thirty. There was a slight breeze, and the rustling of the dead bushes made me jumpy.

"You don't think somebody could have gotten to Sheriff Easterly last night, do you?"

Frank looked worried, but he put on a brave face. "Easterly's smart. I'm sure he wouldn't tell anybody else what we were thinking."

That didn't make me feel any better. If somebody was killing people to keep them from getting at the truth, suppose they got to Easterly? We leaned against the back of the Explorer, and I checked my watch every thirty seconds or so.

At nine-forty-five the sheriff's cruiser pulled up, and I could feel Frank's relief alongside my own. Easterly got out, and we all met next to the Explorer.

"Tomas Blackthorne raises hound dogs," he said, "and some of them are trained as cadaver dogs. I asked him to meet us here with a couple of his best hounds." He looked at his watch. "Zig is coming too. I thought we should keep this to as few people as possible."

We nodded. It had come down to this. Looking for a body in the woods. A body that had been buried forty years ago.

Even though the aroma of pine was still strong, the woods looked less menacing. I tried to conjure up the feeling of the night before, but it didn't work. My brain was focused in the daylight now, and things didn't seem quite as sinister as they had. Maybe we were wrong.

I fidgeted, wanting to get on with it. Finally, a pickup truck pulled in. Dr. Zigler got out of the passenger seat and a big bull of a man exited the driver's side and opened the tailgate. Three hound dogs jumped down and circled the truck, barking and sniffing.

"Come here, Doc," the big man said. At first, I thought he was talking to Dr. Zigler, but then I saw him gesture toward the dogs. The biggest of the three obediently trotted to him and sat. "Sleepy, Bashful, get over here."

Easterly introduced us, and Tomas Blackthorne looked on as his dogs sniffed at us and enjoyed a few minutes of pats and ear-scratching.

Easterly explained to the big man what we were looking for.

"Forty years is a long time," Blackthorne said. "I don't know if the dogs will find anything, but these are the best I have. May as well give it a shot."

Easterly nodded. "Thanks, Tomas." Then he turned to Frank. "Where should we start?"

Frank swept his hand across the woods. "It's not a real big area, so we should be able to cover it in less than an hour." He pointed down the path. "Let's assume Lacey was close to the path when someone arrived. If somebody is buried out here, it probably isn't too far from the path. Let's cover fifty yards on either side."

"We'll start here," Easterly said, "and go up the west side. Tomas, you lead with your dogs, and the rest of us will come behind."

"What are we looking for?" I asked.

Easterly turned to me. "Back east when I was a deputy, we sometimes found bodies buried in parks decades later. There was usually something different about the grass or the bushes right around where the body was."

"A dead body will decay and actually provide nutrients to the soil," Dr. Zigler said. "But this long after death, it's doubtful we'll see any significant difference."

We set off. Tomas walked with his dogs, and I heard him directing them. The rest of us followed, walking farther out and looking for that telltale evidence of a body. We paraded down the side of the path until it ended at the cliff.

"No go," Tomas said.

I felt my eagerness wane. Maybe this was one of those crazy ideas you have at night but it looks completely different in the morning. Maybe there was no body. Maybe Lacey really had fallen over that cliff. And maybe bikers had killed Sinclair thinking he had some great treasure they were going to steal.

My head was spinning with all kinds of ideas when I heard Frank's voice. "Let's try the other side."

We all headed to the other side of the path and started the trek back toward the farmhouse. The dogs were covering the strip of land closest to the path. Easterly and Blackthorne were staying with the dogs.

Frank, Dr. Zigler, and I were out wider, weaving in and out among the trees and looking for the unusual. Something that didn't seem to fit.

All three of us saw it at the same time. No more than twenty feet ahead, a little clearing. Big enough to bury a body in.

Dr. Zigler called, "Tomas, can you bring your dogs over here?"

The dogs yelped and rushed around us. When they got on top of the area, they paused, sniffing and yipping. We stood around it like statues. Instinctively, we knew what lay under that ground, and it was a moment of horror mixed with a desire to show our respect for what we were about to uncover.

We had buried one human being yesterday, and today we were about to bring one back from the grave.

Chapter 43

Lacey's Star

Two days after we found a body in the woods, I borrowed Dolly's CR-V and drove over to visit the McCochran sisters. Frank had asked me to interview them to find out what they knew about Jane Satterfield. Lois and Halcyon welcomed me back to their home with open arms and warm peach pie. I was beginning to think I should move to Balmoral County.

They reminisced for a while about Sinclair and Lacey. Then I broke the news to them about a woman's body being discovered in the same forest Lacey used to play in.

"Who was it?" Lois asked. Her blue eyes looked like X-rays trying to bore into my brain.

I took a deep breath. "Dental records show it was a girl named Jane Satterfield. She was apparently murdered by a blow to the head. Her skull was crushed in one place."

Lois's hand flew to her mouth. "I knew there was something funny going on."

"What do you mean?" I asked.

She sat up straight in her chair. "That girl disappeared about the same time Lacey died. They said she ran away, but it just seemed like too much of a coincidence to believe."

"It's possible she was the princess Lacey thought was being carried into the woods to be put to sleep," I said. "Now all we have to do is find the prince."

Halcyon gasped. "You mean the note really did have something to do with a murder?" She turned pale, and I thought she might faint.

"I'd like to learn more about Jane Satterfield," I said.

Halcyon looked at Lois and the two of them exchanged a silent message. There was something they weren't telling me.

"It's important that you tell me everything you know," I said, trying to sound like an officer of the law who was in command of the situation. But without Frank there, I was flying solo, and I wasn't sure I was doing my job the way he would have done it.

"We don't like to talk ill of the dead," Lois said and looked down at her hands that were clasped tightly in her lap.

I raised my eyebrows. "I understand that, but Jane Satterfield may have been murdered. Whatever you have to say about her, she didn't deserve that."

Halcyon glanced at her sister, then back at me. "You may as well know," she said. "There's a lot of gossip even way out here in the middle of nowhere." She shook her head. "People said Jane was a girl with loose morals."

"She was sleeping around?" I asked.

Lois blushed. "That's what people said."

"Do you know who she was involved with?"

Lois shrugged. "She was in high school. I expect those boys took advantage of her—you know how boys that age are. Especially with a girl who might be, well, weak in that area."

"Who said these things?"

Halcyon reached over and patted my knee. "You may not have a lot of experience with small-town living, dear, but word starts somewhere, and pretty soon everybody is saying the same thing. Who knows where it all started?"

Lois took a tissue out from under her sleeve. "They said Jane ran away because her mother was hard on her."

Halcyon nodded. "Jane's mother worked as a waitress in the Shoalton Cafe."

"And her father?"

"There was no father," Lois responded. "People said the mother got pregnant somewhere back east when she was a teenager and ended up here." She did that clicking thing with her tongue. "Like mother, like daughter."

"Do you know where her mother is now?" I asked.

"After Jane disappeared, her mother moved away. I don't know if anybody knows where she went." Lois crossed her ankles.

Halcyon stopped rocking. "Maybe you could check with Bob Jessop. He would have been about the same age as Jane Satterfield, and he probably knew her. He might have an idea who the murderer could be, being a sheriff and all."

We sat in silence for a few seconds. Then Lois raised her hand like she was in school. "Oh, by the way," she said, and her face brightened. "We remembered something about Lacey's story after you left the other night."

"What's that?"

"Remember, you asked about the cross that was drawn at the end of the sentence?" Halcyon said.

"Yes. You said Lacey must have drawn it."

Lois nodded vigorously and stuck the tissue back under her sleeve. "We remembered Lacey had drawn a star for us once. She was trying to copy the star I cut into my peach pie crust, but she couldn't draw very well, so it came out like a cross."

"You think she was trying to draw a star?" I asked.

"Maybe." Halcyon looked at her sister. "Now that we told you, it seems kind of silly, but it's the only explanation we could come up with."

"Did she say anything about a star?" I asked.

Lois leaned toward me. "I've been going over that day in my mind ever since you left. I think Lacey may have said there was a star. I took it to mean she was out there after dark."

Halcyon's face transformed into a big smile. "And we found the picture of Lacey that we told you about." She jumped up from her rocking chair and pointed to the mantel where there was a picture leaning against the candlesticks.

I walked over and took the picture down. The little girl looking directly at the camera appeared to be about seven or eight years old. She wore a brown dress and red shoes. Her dark hair was straight and cut in a pageboy just at her chin. She wasn't smiling, but her head was tilted a little, as if she was examining the person taking the picture. She looked exactly the way I had pictured her in my mind.

Halcyon stood at my side. "She wasn't a pretty child, but she had something special about her."

"Is this the dress you made for her?" I asked Halcyon.

"Yes." She leaned over and pointed to the white collar on the child's dress. "I bought that lace in town and I told her it was special Chantilly lace that only very good children had. She ran to Lois and showed her the dress and said, 'Look at my lace! Look at my lace!' as if I had given her a million dollars." Halcyon wiped at her eyes with her handkerchief.

"And this is what she was a wearing the day she died?"

"Yes," Lois said." She touched the photo. "They found one of the red shoes on the side of that cliff where they said she fell." She turned away.

My phone played "Fly Me to the Moon." It was Frank. I took the call and nodded as the sisters looked on. I told him what the

McCochran sisters had said about Bob Jessop being around the same age as Jane Satterfield.

When I ended the call, both sisters were leaning toward me as if they were ready to catch whatever information I would throw out.

"I have to go," I said. "Frank says he and Sheriff Easterly are going to drive over to talk to Bob Jessop about the case." I stuffed my phone into my pants pocket. "I'm going to meet them at Sheriff Jessop's office."

Halcyon placed her small hand on my arm. "Be careful, dear. I have bad vibes about all of this."

Lois harrumphed. "Don't start that hocus-pocus stuff, Halcyon." She put her hand on my other arm. "I don't have any vibes, but our old daddy used to say, 'Where there's smoke, there's fire.'" She squeezed my arm. "Doesn't take a wizard to know that where there's a murder, bad things are bound to be happening. Be careful."

"Thanks for your concern." I hoisted my bag over my shoulder. "But I'm just going to the sheriff's office. That's probably one of the safest places in the world."

Chapter 44

The Last Piece of the Puzzle

My breath was coming fast and hard as I drove toward Willard County. We were close to the finish line, and my heart was pounding. We knew Sinclair was murdered and Jane Satterfield was murdered. If we could identify Jane's murderer, we'd know who killed Lacey Alderson. And that would close the circle. Bob Jessop was our best hope for a lead.

Frank told me Sheriff Easterly had informed Bob Jessop that we had discovered a body, but I wasn't sure if Jessop knew the identity.

I pulled into the small gravel lot in front of Sheriff Jessop's office and parked next to the sheriff's cruiser. The same pickup truck was there that we had seen before. I assumed it belonged to Mannie Jessop. Good. Maybe the older sheriff could help us fill in the blanks.

Bob Jessop was sitting alone in the front office, and he looked up with an expression of anticipation on his face. Did he know?

"Good morning, Cassie." He greeted me with a wide smile. "Sheriff Easterly told me you'd be stopping by. Apparently, we're going to have a powwow about the body they found."

"Yes. Frank told me to meet them here."

"In that case, maybe I should make a pot of coffee. I expect we're all going to need some." He stood. "Have a seat. I'll be back in a sec."

He left to go to the small kitchen, and I walked around the office to calm my jittery nerves. I roamed along the edges of the room, looking at the citations, articles, and photos that lined the walls.

I stopped in front of the big picture of a young Bob Jessop standing next to his father at the back of the brown pickup truck. Mannie Jessop said Bob was eighteen when that picture was taken, and the McCochran sisters said he may have known Jane Satterfield. I stared at the image of Bob, a vigorous young man with movie-star good looks, and I wondered just how well he knew her.

There was a date on the picture that made me flinch when I noticed it. October 1970. That was just a couple of months after Lacey died.

I examined the faces of Bob and Mannie in the picture. Bob looked happy, but Mannie looked overjoyed, like he was proud enough to pop the buttons on his flannel shirt. I remembered what he said about how wonderful it was to have a good son.

As my eyes dropped to look at the elk that was lying at their feet, something caught my attention. The license plate on the truck had the word "WILLARD" at the top, indicating it was a Willard County tag. Most of it was visible since the men were standing on each side of it. But there was something else. The right side of the license plate was partially hidden by Mannie Jessop's leg, and there was something there that I couldn't make out.

Bob came out of the kitchen, wiping his hands on a paper towel. "It'll take a few more minutes for the coffee." He stood beside me.

"This is a great picture," I said.

"That was a special day," he said. "Everything in that picture is important to me. Bagging that elk, my dad being so proud. Even that old brown pickup was special." He grinned. "Dad let me have it when I got my driver's license. I must have put a million miles on that old truck."

"I was trying to figure out what this thing is on the license plate. Something's behind your father's leg." I pointed. "Are there more numbers on the tag?"

He leaned toward the photo to see what I was talking about. "Oh, right there?" He touched the picture. "That's a star."

"A star?" My mouth fell open.

"Yeah. There's one on all the sheriff's vehicles, even the personal ones." He turned away. "I'm going to check on the coffee."

I called after him. "I need to step outside and make a call. I'll be back in a second."

I left the office, walked outside to the parking lot, and stopped behind the pickup truck. My heart turned into an icy fist when I saw the emblem of a sheriff's star on the right side of the license plate. The puzzle began to take shape in my mind.

I took the phone out of my pocket and called Frank's number, but it rolled over to voice mail, so I left a message. "I'm at Jessop's office. I know who killed Jane Satterfield."

I hung up and walked back inside with my heart whamming against my rib cage. I stared again at the picture of the hunters in front of their kill, and I felt a righteous anger pulse through every cell in my body, all the way to my fingertips. I hit the Record icon on my phone and laid it on top of the shelf under the picture.

Bob came out holding two cups of steaming coffee and placed them on the desk. "If you think you'd like to try elk hunting, I'd be happy to take you up on the mountain any time you like."

Mr. Congeniality. Daddy's golden-haired boy. Handsome enough to be a prince, and the last person you'd ever suspect. More pieces of the puzzle dropped into place, and I turned to face him. He was smiling at me with a big, toothy grin that reminded me of a wolf. "It was you," I blurted out.

His eyes widened, but he was still smiling. "What do you mean?"

"Someone buried a girl in the woods forty years ago. When the murderer found out that Lacey Alderson had witnessed it, he murdered her too."

"Cassie, I think you're trying to fit two incidents together. There's no evidence that Lacey Alderson was murdered, and we don't know the identity of the body they found."

"Yes, we do."

He looked startled.

"Frank just came from the coroner's office. Dental records show the dead woman is Jane Satterfield." I felt my mouth curve into a sneer. "She was pregnant."

He wobbled and leaned on the desk to steady himself.

"It was your baby, wasn't it? Did she demand that you marry her? I'm guessing you murdered her and buried her in the woods, but you didn't count on a little girl witnessing it."

He stood up straight and put his left hand on his gun. "You're crazy. You don't know what you're talking about."

"You know what gave it away?" I gestured to the picture on the wall. "It was the star on the license plate of the pickup truck of yours. The sheriff's star. Lacey said she saw the prince bring the princess in the wild wood. She was misreading the word 'Willard' on the license plate. She thought it said "Wildwood." And then she drew a cross. But it wasn't a cross to her. It was the star on the license plate." I felt light-headed.

Bob Jessop's eyes bulged.

My body was stiff with tension. I took a breath and pointed at him. "You killed Jane Satterfield."

"That isn't true." His shoulders sagged, but his hand was still on his gun. "I loved Jane, but she was only sixteen years old. We never had sexual relations." He looked as if he were pleading for me to believe him. "My dad read the riot act to me a million times about not having sex with an underage girl. He told me I could wind up in jail if I did."

"So maybe you found out she was pregnant by another man and killed her."

"You don't know what you're talking about. I would never have hurt Jane." He was still fingering his gun, but he hadn't removed it from the holster. I thought of the .38 revolver sitting in the glove compartment of Dolly's CR-V.

I pointed to the picture on the wall. My voice got so loud I almost didn't realize it belonged to me. "Well, somebody drove that pickup truck into the woods."

Bob's voice ratcheted up to match mine. "That's nonsense. The only other person who had keys to that pickup—"

He stopped so suddenly, the air seemed to freeze around us. We didn't move but gawked at each other. We both knew the answer. Neither of us had seen Mannie Jessop walk out from the back of the building.

"I'm the only other person who had keys to that truck," he said amiably. "What's all this about?"

Bob stood like stone, staring at his father.

Mannie didn't seem to notice. "You're not accusing me of murder, are you Cassie?"

It was as if someone had pulled the curtain back and all the players took their places in front of me. There was Jane Satterfield, a frightened sixteen-year-old girl telling a man she was pregnant with his child. A man who couldn't afford for anyone else to know his secret. A man who had the means to kill Jane, bury her in the woods, and leave some of her clothes at a truck stop to mislead anybody who was searching for her. I knew the answer before I asked the question. "Did you murder her, sheriff?"

Mannie plastered a thin smile on his face. "I'm not going to take offense to you, Cassie. I know you're just trying to make sense out of a terrible tragedy, but you're a new deputy. You're just accusing everybody in sight, hoping something will stick."

"Did you kill her?"

"Listen to what you're saying, girl. I'm an officer of the law. I've spent my life upholding the law. Ask anybody in Willard County." He gave a dismissive wave of the hand. "That girl was a runaway. Everybody knew it." He looked at his son and shook his head. "Bob, this is why we should never give a badge to a woman. They deal in emotion, not fact."

From the corner of my eye, I could see Bob Jessop's face turning dark red. He knew.

Mannie hooked his thumbs in his waistband like he was getting ready to lay some kind of "aw, shucks" line on me. "I heard what you said about her being pregnant. I guess that little floozy got herself in trouble."

"She wasn't a floozy, Dad." Bob took a step toward his father.

Mannie held his hand out as if to stop the thoughts that were forming in Bob's mind. "I know you were sweet on her, son, but I talked to her mother and some others in the community, and I learned she was sleeping around and talking about getting out of this hick town. I figured she finally hitched a ride with some trucker and made her escape. Sunderman said they found some of her things at a truck stop." He shook his head. "I'm sorry, Bob. You never wanted to hear about Jane's lack of moral character. I tried to shield you from the truth these many years."

Mannie turned his attention back to me. "I hope they find the killer, but it's been so long."

Everything clicked. "Sinclair told you he had some kind of proof that his sister was murdered, and he left it at Uncle Charlie's farm. So you killed him, and then you hired those ex-cons to find the proof Sinclair thought he had." I huffed. "Was it the handkerchief you were after? You must have dropped it the day you buried Jane."

Both Jessop men stared at me.

"You made it all up, didn't you?" My words were coming out fast, trying to keep up with my thoughts. "There were no bikers at a campsite, and Sinclair wasn't drinking. You set up the scene to look like he had committed suicide. Then you lied about all of it to throw us off. " I took a deep breath as the last piece of the puzzle fell into place.

Mannie looked at his son again and shook his head. "I guess you have to be a woman to come up with a fairy tale like that." He sneered at me. "Besides, you can't prove anything. You don't have any witnesses to who killed Sinclair or attacked your uncle. And you sure don't have any witnesses to who killed Jane Satterfield."

"We do have a witness." I stared him down. "The baby," I said. "The baby will tell us who the father is."

Red blotches appeared on Mannie's face.

I lifted my chin. "The baby's DNA will tell the story."

Mannie's mouth turned down. "I doubt you can find enough DNA left in a six-month-old fetus after forty years to tell you anything."

I raised my eyebrows in mock surprise. "How did you know she was six months pregnant?"

It was as if someone had hit Pause on a video. The three of us didn't move for several seconds while the light of truth spread over us. All of us knew exactly what had taken place in that scrawny patch of dirt and trees forty years ago.

Mannie Jessop's face had gone scarlet. "Kill her, Bob," his voice brayed out. "She comes in here accusing us of murder. She's obviously trying to make a name for herself by this crazy talk. We can set it up to look like she attacked us."

The hair stood up on the back of my neck. I wanted to turn and run, but my feet felt like they were nailed to the floor. I looked to Bob for help. He was hunched over his desk, and his shoulders began to shake. He was crying.

Mannie looked at his son, then turned to me. His lips curled back over his teeth in a snarl. "You little ..." With his left hand, he drew a gun from his side holster and pointed it at my chest.

I heard Frank's voice scream, "Cassie!" I turned toward the sound just as a gunshot exploded. Then a second one went off. In the small office, they sounded like cannons.

Chapter 45

The Cemetery

Sinclair Alderson
July 1, 1950 - August 11, 2010
Devoted Brother

A little rain fell that morning. Lois said it was the first they'd had in years. Halcyon said God was showing his mercy.

We stood in a semicircle around the grave after Sinclair's tombstone was put in place. Brother and sister lay side by side in the Eternal Peace Cemetery. Uncle Charlie had gotten the stone carver to make matching headstones for Sinclair's and Lacey's graves. I made a mental note to stop by the mason's shop and compliment him on his work.

When no family members were found for Jane Satterfield, Uncle Charlie purchased a plot on the other side of Lacey's grave for Jane's body to be interred after the coroner completed all his work. In the end, Sinclair, Lacey, Jane, and Jane's child, all murdered by Mannie Jessop, would lie together.

Ruddy Buchanan and his sister, Shirley, joined the same small group that had gathered for Sinclair's burial two weeks earlier. Mannie Jessop, of course, was not in attendance.

Bob Jessop had resigned his position as sheriff, and I heard rumors that Easterly had made a few calls suggesting Frank should apply for the position. I had a feeling Ruddy wouldn't want to lose his star deputy, and he stood on the other side of Frank.

The McCochran sisters had picked a bouquet of yellow and white wildflowers and placed them on the grave. Lois told me they were called blanket flowers. We needed them. The shock and sadness of the past week had drained us of our spirits, and the flowers' sweet aroma was a welcome comfort.

Lois stood straight as an arrow in her black slacks that rose a little above the ankles, her hair pulled back into a bun. Halcyon was beside her, leaning on her sister's arm and wiping tears with a blue handkerchief that matched her dark blue dress. I'm sure she made both herself.

Greg and Dolly held hands on the other side of the grave. He would occasionally glance down at her with just enough of a smile to make his scar stand out. I had never seen Dolly look so beautiful. She wore a plain black dress and covered her hair with a black veil. I'm afraid I'm going to lose my roommate.

Sheriff Easterly stood at the foot of the grave. His face bore the weight of the search for truth, and he was beginning to resemble a western lawman. He was even wearing cowboy boots.

Uncle Charlie stood next to me, clutching Lacey's Bible. Frank was on my other side.

I had learned a difficult lesson. The truth does not always taste sweet, and I had struggled with the bitterness of what we had uncovered ever since that day in the Willard County Sheriff's Office.

Pastor John stood behind the newly laid gravestone with his tattered Bible in his hands and read from the book of John. "I am the resurrection and the life. Whoever believes in me, though he die, yet shall he live, and everyone who lives and believes in me shall never die." He looked a lot older to me than he had when he first knocked on Uncle Charlie's door that day. I think his beard had more gray in it.

Pastor John finished his eulogy and called on Uncle Charlie to say a few words. Uncle walked behind the gravestone and faced us. He opened Lacey's Bible and flipped a few pages.

"I've been doing some reading," he said and tapped on the Bible, "about a man who was born blind." I knew he was talking about the book of John, chapter nine, my favorite story about a blind man who was miraculously healed.

"Sinclair Alderson was a man like that," he said. "He wasn't a bad man, but he had been raised in a family with no bonds of faith, and he'd left that family in anger. When he came home from Vietnam, his life was almost destroyed when he discovered his little sister, whom he adored, was dead."

Uncle Charlie's eyes moistened. "Sinclair Alderson was as blind as any man ever was, until one day a good man found him in a ditch and opened his eyes." He gave a brief nod to Pastor John.

"And then Sinclair opened this." He held up Lacey's little Bible. "And he found something that made him want to seek the truth about Lacey's death. You all know the rest.

"Sinclair told Pastor John he wanted two things. He wanted peace, and he wanted justice for Lacey. In the end, both of those prayers were answered." Uncle placed his hand on top of the tombstone. "Rest in peace, my friend. I'm glad you found your way home."

The McCochran sisters insisted we all congregate at their house, and most of the group left. An unsmiling Ruddy Buchanan touched my arm and asked me to stay behind for a minute. Frank stood with me while Shirley waited off to the side.

"You made a mistake, Cassie," Ruddy said, and his dark eyebrows knitted together. "You went into a dangerous situation without a gun, without backup, and accused someone of murder. It could have ended very badly for you." He nodded toward Frank. "And for Deputy White."

I didn't realize until that moment how much I had wanted Ruddy Buchanan's approval. Disappointment was etched in the frown he wore, and I was ashamed. "I'm sorry, Sheriff Buchanan," I said. "I acted out of anger. It was stupid." I felt tears sting my eyes. I reached into my purse and pulled out the deputy badge he had pinned on me a couple of weeks before. I held it out to him. "I knew I wasn't qualified to wear this."

He looked down at my hand but didn't move. His eyes softened. "None of us are qualified, Cassie," he said quietly, "but we learn from our mistakes, and that's one you won't make again." He emitted a sigh, the first sign of emotion I had ever seen from him. "A lot of evil was committed here over the years. If it hadn't been for you, we may never have found that girl's body and never have put the picture together. Justice would not have been served." He almost smiled. "You deserve a medal, Cassie."

His voice returned to its command level. "I know you're planning to stay with your uncle until he regains his strength. I'd like you to remain on my team during that time."

I felt Frank move closer. "I'd like that," I said.

"Then hold onto that badge, young lady, and report to me at eight o'clock Monday morning. We'll see what we can work out."

"Yes, sir."

Shirley smiled, and Frank put his arm around me.

Sheriff Buchanan put his Stetson on and turned to go. "C'mon Shirl, let's go get some of that pie everybody's raving about."

Shirley gave a salute. "Coming, Cap'n." She rolled her eyes at me and followed him.

Frank and I trailed behind and stopped by the open grave that would house the body of Sheriff Jessop. A marker was already in place.

Rayman (Mannie) Jessop
April 21, 1934 - August 24, 2010

"I hear Bob Jessop resigned as sheriff the day after the shooting," I said.

"That's right."

"Will he be charged with a crime?" I asked.

"I doubt it. He was in his rights to shoot Mannie since he was acting to protect you."

I had been having nightmares. They were almost perfect reenactments of that day in Bob Jessop's office when the truth of Jane Satterfield's murder hit him and he turned his gun on his own father.

Frank's hand stiffened. "Ruddy was right. You shouldn't have gone into that office and accused the Jessops without your gun." He shook his head.

I stopped and picked up a vase that had fallen over by an old grave. "I know, but all I could think about was that picture the McCochran sisters showed me. Little Lacey was wearing the brown dress Halcyon made for her and the red shoes Lois bought. Really, Frank, there was something about that picture that just about tore my heart in two."

"Yeah. I saw the picture. After the shooting, they got it framed and put it right in the middle of their mantel."

"When I saw the star on the sheriff's truck and put the whole thing together, I was in a state of fury, but at least I had the presence of mind to hit the Record button on my phone. I kept thinking of that child being pushed over the cliff because one evil man wanted to keep his dirty little secret." I put my arm around Frank's waist. "You should have seen the look on Bob Jessop's face when I accused him. When it dawned on both of us at the same time that it was Mannie, I kind of lost it."

"Yeah. I listened to the recording from your phone. I never realized you could shout that loud." He put his finger under my chin and lifted my face. "Remind me never to make you mad."

In reality, Frank had saved my life. Mannie Jessop had drawn his gun and was ready to put a bullet in my heart when Frank charged in. Mannie swung his arm around to shoot Frank. Two shots were fired almost simultaneously. Frank was hit in the arm before he could get his own gun out of the holster. "Flesh wound," he called it when we got him to the hospital. "Now Charlie and I are twins."

Bob Jessop's bullet went into the side of his father's head.

"Did the State Bureau of Investigation find anything when they searched Mannie's home?" I asked.

Frank nodded. "They found a couple of photos showing Mannie with a handkerchief that had a red letter R embroidered on it. His wife is cooperating. She said Mannie's mother used to sew those for him because she was so proud of her son."

We walked on slowly. "Dr. Zigler got the DNA results," Frank said. "Mannie Jessop was indeed the father of Jane Satterfield's child." He sighed. "It was a boy."

I felt an electric shock go through me. "He killed his own son."

Frank looked down into my eyes. "It's ironic, isn't it? He killed his son and his other son killed him." His jaw clenched. He took a deep breath and pulled me closer. We stood for a minute and then began the walk to his car.

"I was thinking about what you asked me," he said.

I raised my eyebrows. "What did I ask?"

"About whether my mother would have wanted to settle for second-best just to get a few more years in this life."

"Ah." I stopped and looked up at him. "What did you decide?"

"My mother once told me that my dad was her destiny."

"That's a beautiful thing to say."

"Yeah. I wish you had known them, Cassie."

"Me too."

We walked over to the fence that bordered the cemetery and Frank put his hand behind my head, pulled me to him, and kissed me.

"I sure hope this arm heals soon. I need both hands," he said and grinned down at me.

"You're doing pretty good with just one."

"Will you have dinner with me tonight?" he asked.

I put my hand on my hip and a skeptical expression on my face. "Suppose you stand me up?"

"I know this little Italian restaurant in Boise. We can fly up there and make an evening of it."

"Only if I'm pilot-in-command," I said.

"No problem." He lifted his left arm a little. "I'm on medical leave." He kissed me again. "And I need tender loving care."

"I'll think about it," I said as he opened the door to the car for me to get in the driver's seat. "But first I have something I want to try out."

Frank walked around and got in the passenger door. "What?"

No use telling him about the eyelash curler.

THE END

About the Author

Thank you, dear reader, for having read *Lacey's Star*. If you liked it, you may also enjoy the original short story, *Lady Pilot-in-Command*, which inspired this novel. You can download it free on my website at kaydibianca.com.

You may also like the books in my other series, *The Watch Mysteries*. Those include *The Watch on the Fencepost*, *Dead Man's Watch* and *Time After Tyme*. These books feature half-sisters Kathryn Frasier and Cece Goldman as they tackle cryptic clues and deadly villains while navigating life's many challenges. I would especially appreciate it if you would leave a review on Amazon, Goodreads, or one of the other book sites for any of my books that you've enjoyed.

If you want to know more about me, I'm a former software developer and IT manager who retired to a life of mystery. I am having the time of my life writing novels and short stories. I also write a bi-weekly blog post on the Kill Zone Blog.

As if that weren't enough, I've been blessed with a long marriage to a good man with whom I've shared many interests, and together we raised a wonderful son. Frank and I are deeply thankful for the blessings God has bestowed on our family.

One of my great pleasures in life is problem-solving, and I think that's why I enjoy writing mysteries. Everybody loves a good whodunit, and I like creating puzzles for readers to solve.

You may have guessed from this book that I'm a licensed pilot.

Although I'm no longer active, the thrill of lifting off the surface of the Earth and soaring into blue sky has never left me.

And then there's running. You can often find me at a track, on the treadmill, or at a park near our home. The mantra *Never Give Up* that Kathryn repeats in the running scenes of my *Watch* mystery books is dear to me.

I'd love to hear from you. You can connect with me on my website at:

kaydibianca.com

or through one of the social media links at the end of this page.

In the meantime, stay safe, enjoy life, and read good books.

facebook.com/kay.dibianca

twitter.com/Kdibianca

instagram.com/kdibianca

Made in the USA
Columbia, SC
07 January 2024

29306519R10137